SHIT JUST GOT REAL

THE EXECUTIVE HOMEBOY

CONTENTS

AUTHOR PAGE

The Executive Homeboy is an award winning, Urban Novel Author with the natural gift of creative writing. He's the Chief Executive Officer of the Atlanta based investment company, Farm Houze Group LLC. For more information on the Author **visit: www.theexecutivehomeboy.com**

PROLOGUE

*F*ace to face with Houston's Saturday night skies, Triple J, sat relaxing outdoors in a soft cushioned rose red patio chair. The weather was even tempered, perfect for relaxing outside on a Saturday night. He and his wife, Mrs. Jessica Reeves-Johnson, were supposed to be traveling under the radar, but she picked the number one hotel in the city of Houston to spend the night.

Spoiled to her core, Jessica refused to sleep in anything less than the five-star rating hotel. So tonight, they're spending it at the hotel Granduca Houston. Usually when they traveled, Triple J made sure they were protected by at least thirty members of his Ape's and Wolves crew. Mainly members from the hunters, his cleanup crew, but tonight, it's just the two of them.

Triple J knew he wasn't supposed to move in such a manner, because it put them both in physical danger. The streets don't have a heart and a big fish like Triple J had enemies they didn't even know existed.

The trip to Texas was scheduled as a day trip—fly in,

check on her grandfather, then fly right back to Atlanta, but during their visit, Bianca, Jessica's favorite cousin, showed up out of the blue. What a coincidence it was Bianca was also there to surprise Grandpa at the same time that they did.

"Growing up, Jessica and Bianca were inseparable," their grandfather told Triple J. "And even though they're cousins, you would think they were twins. Can you believe this one year, they both sent me the same shirt for Christmas and the only difference in the whole gift was the name on the top of the box? They think just alike," Grandpa chuckled.

Triple J learned that this is the first time in five years that they are seeing each other, and the surprise visit had them super excited. Jessica had been super busy with Triple J and the day-to-day operations in their real estate group, while Bianca had been engulfed in her work at a high-paying government job she had out in Cali.

Jessica never told Triple J exactly what Bianca did because she knew how he felt about Feds. All he knew was she traveled a lot. For Jessica, the trip to see grandpa was bittersweet. She loved them both and wished for them all to hang out, but Triple J couldn't. What most people didn't know was for major players in the streets like he was, shit got real. Crossing over state lines into other territories for business or vacation, meant he must check in. The rule stated that if one was traveling outside of his approved travel area, he must notify the family's Chief of Security who covered the territory in which he visited, of the departure. Once he did so, the family's Chief of Security would grant permission or rejection before he arrived. Triple J had done neither and Jessica acted as if she didn't understand why he stressed that they had to remain low-key before they'd left Atlanta.

"When we travel outside of the United States, the government requires us to have visas. The streets are the same way," he told her.

Just to make this trip, had already cost him 170k in flight expenses. To keep it off all stations, he had to make a couple of rich calls and settled on a business deal he had no plans of settling for another month. The Learjet was loaned out by one of his personal business associates so they could bypass airport TSA and arrive there under aliases.

Pouting because she couldn't spend the night out with her favorite two, Jessica pranced around their hotel suite with her lips poking out, swinging her backside in every direction from underneath her turquoise lace boy shorts. From his view, Triple J thought, *she looks like one of those big stank booty strippers at a hole in the wall strip club that ain't made no money all night.*

Can you say attitude!

He never liked seeing her upset, but he did think the walk was kind of cute as she stumped her way into the bathroom.

While Jessica was getting dolled up, Triple J was enjoying stress-free moments before he heard her voice again.

"Daddy!" she called out, walking from the apartment sized bathroom. "Does this dress look slutty?" she asked.

Triple J turned towards her and walked through the sliding glass door. Standing in front of him, he stared in amazement.

Oh my God. She looks like a beauty queen, he thought.

Jessica only wore the best and if she were into pageants, she could have easily won Miss America. Modeling for him, she wore a purple custom-made Michael Kors, gold studded uneven hem dress that cut knee level. She stood offset with

3

her right leg slightly advanced, showing off the contour of her body.

Dressed elegantly with all of the matching Michael Kors gold accessories, necklace, bracelet, and time watch, she gave him a cold shiver that raced across every vertebrate of his spine. Styled by H0n3y @HoneyLegacy in Atlanta, Jessica stayed dressed in only the best of attire each time she stepped out, putting on for her city.

As Triple J continued to stare her down, wild thoughts ran through his mind.

It's like God created her just for me, he thought.

Hands down, Mrs. Jessica Reeves-Johnson was made for a king and just by the luck of the draw, he got her. Running his eyes across her body, Triple J wondered why she asked if her dress looked slutty. Honey's Nation's seamstress hemmed it perfectly, hugging her curves like a mother with her child for the first time.

Triple J saw nothing wrong, but if the U.S. Department of Transportation inspectors saw her, they would. An emergency order would be sent to the State Governor, forcing them to put up warning signs around Jess because the curves ahead were sharp.

"You look beautiful baby," he said. "Why would you even ask me do you look slutty?" Triple J asked as he walked up to her licking his lips. Jessica giggled as Triple J reached out grabbing her right hand.

"No, I'm serious, daddy. Does it look slutty?" she asked him for a second time.

Head held high, she stared at a 45-degree angle, showing off her beautiful jawline as she waited for him to respond. Rocking from side to side, she mimicked a runway model that would pause at the edge of the stage.

"You're beautiful and it's beautiful," he said with amazement in his eyes. "It fits you, Love. I can see Mrs. Michelle Obama wanting to wear this dress after seeing you in it."

"Really? You think the First Lady would wanna wear a dress like me?"

"Without a shadow of doubt! She won't look as good as you do, but absolutely." he said, lifting her hand above her head before spinning her slowly like a ballerina.

Jessica blushed as she turned, harder than he'd ever seen her blush. Much harder than she did when they had first met.

She broke away from his grip and lifted both hands up, grabbing around his neck. Raising on the tip of her toes, she lifted up to his lips and kissed him with her luscious lips passionately. Twirling in circles, she caught his lips between her teeth, biting down slightly before she released him. Licking up his face as she pulled away, she left a wet spot on the tip of his nose.

"Daddy, I love you so much," she said. "You've always made me feel special, even on a night like tonight."

"I know you want me to come, but really I can't," he said to her.

Jessica interlocked fingers with him and they both stared silently deep into each other's eyes. Her big and beautiful brown eyes gave a glow so beautiful that Triple J lit up each time he stared into them.

Holding hands, they both recognized that their love for one another was stronger than either of them understood. Their connection was deep and reached way into the crevices of their souls.

Jessica's phone rang, interrupting their romantic moment and they both knew who was on the other end of the line.

"Hey, B," Jessica said as she answered the phone. "Okay, I'm on the way down now sis," she continued after a slight pause.

Grabbing the extra magazine to his pistol from between the sofa's cushion, Triple J quickly slid it in his back pocket as she slid on her heels. "Will you ride down the elevator with me?" she asked after checking her makeup one last time.

"Yeah, baby. You didn't think I was gonna let you ride down by yourself, did you?"

"I don't know. You know you have them street rules you have to follow. Rule number three says you can't walk your wife downstairs or open the car door," she said sarcastically.

"Watch out," Triple J said, brushing off her sarcasm.

Stepping out of the room, they held hands to the elevator. Triple J stepped in behind his wife and placed his back against the wall. Jessica backed up against him, pressing her butt on his lap as they rode down to the lobby.

As the doors opened, Jess gave him three pecks on the lips.

"I love you, daddy," she said before stepping off.

Triple J stayed on the elevator but watched as she walked away.

Her walk away was breathtaking, switching up and down every time she stepped. Jessica knew he was watching because the elevator doors beeped before closing, she twirled around, flung her hair, then smiled as she continued to march away.

"My bitch bad," Triple J thought, as he rode the elevator up alone.

Bored out of his mind, Triple J dozed off after flipping through channels. The suite's door opened, and he quickly grabbed his custom Glock 23 compact .40 cal, aiming its barrel towards the hotel suite's door as it opened.

"Baby, it's me," Jessica said, announcing herself as she walked in.

Triple J lowered his gun and checked his wristwatch for the time, because the night still felt young. He then grabbed his cell phone off the nightstand checking it for any missed calls because he knew Jessica would usually have called or texted, letting him know that she was on her way back, but tonight she didn't.

"Damn, it's just 10:35," he said to himself, but loud enough so she could hear him. It was a sure thing that if they were home, she would have hung out at least until 2:30 or 3:00 AM.

Something's not right, Triple J thought to himself.

"What's up, pretty lady?" he asked as he walked up to Jessica stepping out of her shoes," Did you enjoy yourself," he asked.

Jess didn't respond but let out a sigh like she was upset.

"What time do the clubs close out here?" he asked her, looking at his watch again.

"We didn't go to a club. They were all overcrowded, so we just hit up a restaurant, talked and sipped wine," she said with a slight slur in her speech.

"What's wrong, Jessie? Were y'all not having a good time?"

"You don't miss me?" she asked quickly with a hint of anger in her voice.

"Of course, I miss you! I'm just trying to figure out what's got my smile upset. "

"Daddy! We did have a good time. Maybe I came back early because I had to tee-tee," Jessica said with a smirk on her face.

7

With only one heel off, Jessica stood with her legs crossed like a little kid rocking back and forth doing the pee-pee dance.

"You hell," Triple J replied, laughing at her drunkard behavior. "Go pee and don't get none on my floor," he continued, laughing at her move quickly towards the bathroom.Bouncing up and down as she walked in one heel, he stopped her in her tracks outside the bathroom door."Baby, let me help you take off your heel," he said, bending down reaching for her foot being the gentleman that he was.

Deep down though she knew he really loved her and ensuring her safety was his job. No real man would watch his wife continue down the path of disaster and possibly twist her ankle. Triple J returned to the bed and laid back. All night long, he'd been chilling, and his phone surprisingly hadn't rung once, until she got back. The incoming call came from the encrypted telephone app he had for close relatives during emergencies only. So immediately his antennas raised.

"Papa, what's up?" he answered the call quickly, coming from the old man, Pastor James Johnson, Senior.

"Where you at, son?" he asked in a very serious tone.

"Texas with Jess. What's going on?"

"Stay put. Atlanta homicide detectives just came by looking for you."

"Was it just the detectives or the whole team?" Triple J asked.

"Errbody," his father said. "They came deep."

Lost for words Triple J remained silent. His whole world had been shaken up and that's when he knew then,

Shit Just Got Real.

1

For the past few weeks, Triple J had these fucked up feelings in his gut. He sensed things in his life were on the verge of making a turn for the worse. Despite everything positive, he did to repel the negative energy, it just continued to snatch at him.

Now that shit had gotten real, he had to go black and fall clean off the grid. First, he started by destroying his electronic devices. Any and everything with GPS capabilities had to go, including Jessica's phone. As he gathered everything together, Jessica walked out of the bathroom and the BBA ALARM went off.

"It's a Bad Bitch Alert! Bad Bitch Alert!"

Standing in the center of the room floor, Jessica rolled her curvy hips slowly eight or so feet away from the bed. Slowly tracing her hands across her body, she danced with no music like an island girl, in a ruby red lace bra and panties set.

Her hands glided across her body, raining down her hips slowly, as she rolled into smooth choreographed motions. She sent extremely high vibrations across the room as her body swayed.

From the smalls of her back, she pulled out a gold top clear cylinder container. Pressing the container's top, she popped open its cap and began to pour the body oil across the front of her body.

Got damn. My wife is beautiful, Triple J thought to himself as she oiled her body. *She makes brand name strippers look like regular ol' hoochie mama's in a two-dollar whore house.*

His penis got on instant hard, taking no time to reach its erection, as she continued to oil herself down. Beams of heavenly glows illuminated from her body, lighting up the room creating a joyous feeling for the both of them.

As he watched her body sway, relaxation from the hypnosis caused him to fall back onto the bed, bracing on both elbows. Jessica's eyes rolled into her head and she looked like she's escaped into another realm as she continued her strip show. She began a forward motion moving in his direction, still swaying her hips as she began to pop her breast up and down. When she reached the foot of the bed, she paused with her hands twisted above her head.

Unsure of what was coming next, Triple J downed a deep gulp of saliva that had built up in his mouth while he watched her. Jessica opened her eyes and they both stared deep into one another's souls. Lowering herself slightly at the knees, planting soft, short kisses across his neck, Jessica moved to his lips, kissing them too while still swaying. Inserting her hands into his pants, she grabbed a handful and lowered herself all the way to the floor.

On her knees between his legs, Jessica began to flick her tongue out like a snake, before making a lap around her juicy glossed lips. Triple J's, Johnson grew harder, jerking inside his pants as she loosened the drawstring to his pajama joggers.

Flew!

It was like pop goes the weasel with the way his manhood flew out. The sudden reaction caused Jessica's head to jerk back and she smiled. Wasting no time to wrap her big and beautiful lips around the tip of his rocket, lil mama slowly lowered her head, accepting all of him with very little gagging.

Triple J leaned his head back but then a heavy weight tugged at the side of his pants. Almost forgetting the pistol on his waistband, Triple J slowly removed his gat, grabbing it by the black cloth conceal holster. Jessica continued to pleasure him, as he laid it next to them on the nightstand.

As she continued, he bit down on his bottom lip, struggling not to moan aloud. But when Jess turned up the speed, bobbing her head in a higher gear, that all changed.

"Agh, aah, ah. Agh, my God," he yelled out in a soprano voice tone that sounded so inappropriate to him.

If anyone heard that, they would have thought that he was the one getting screwed with how bad it sounded. He did not care, to him it felt good so Jessica continued. Her mouth got wetter and wetter like a water fountain with no drain. Uncontrollable sporadic jerks appeared in his legs and his entire body locked up as large clusters of sperm raced into her mouth.

Triple J loved when she got nasty like this. It was like he was married to a professional porn star. Jessica slurped all of the ejection into her mouth, no spit, no spills, all swallowed. Licking her lips, she raised her head and opened her mouth wide, smacking her tongue before sticking it out to show it was all gone.

Rising up, Jessica lifted her right leg and climbed onto his lap, but he interrupted her plans. Wrapping one arm around her back and sliding the other under her leg, he twisted her to the side, laying her on her back smoothly like an exotic dance move.

A big Kool-Aid smile stretched across her face, as he lifted her legs high into the air. Strategically, he began to place gentle kisses down the center of her abdomen, pausing at her navel. Tickling her, he navigated his tongue around her navel indention, and she pushed his head away as she let out kiddie laughs.

"Wrong hole, fool," she said while trying to force his head lower.

"Oh, my bad. I thought I was on that spot. No wonder I couldn't feel no hair around it," he replied jokingly.

Uncomfortable, half leaning across the bed, he stood to set the table right.

Jessica rubbed between her thick thighs while she waited. Rolling her eyes into the back of her head, she fingered the top of her super soaked panties, pleasing herself as she waited. Triple J watched for a while, stroking his pole as the sexual excitements rushed inside the both of them. He snatched up one of the pillowcases and tied it around his neck like a baby's bib because shit-was about to get real.

Reaching under Jessica's thick thighs, he pulled her to the edge of the bed and fell to his knees. Remembering to give thanks before every meal, he pressed his hands together and began to pray.

"Dear, Heavenly Father. Today I give thanks for this amazingly beautiful meal you have prepared for me today," he began to say, but Jessica interrupted him, giggling and tugging at his ear.

"Stop being silly. That's what's wrong with you. You need some Vitamin V."

"Vitamin V?" he asked after pausing to process what she'd said. "Okay, since you're a nutritionist now, please tell me what Vitamin V's good for?" he asked jokingly.

"Everything!" she yelled. "Now stop being silly and eat this pussy. I bet you know what that's good for."

Triple J nodded his head up and down rapidly, smiling while she forced his head between her thighs. Circling his tongue around her clitoris, he caused her facial lips to quiver while therapeutically manipulating her vaginal lips. Making all kinds of melodic sex sounds, Jess sang out as the ecstasy flow built inside her body, which ignited a fire inside.

"I'm about to cum," she screamed, tensing up as he continued to please her.

And like a bear trap, her legs slammed shut and locked around his head.

The warm fluids erupted from her vagina like lava flowing from a volcano. And Triple J continued to please her, until she forcefully pushed his head away as tears ran from hers.

"I can't take it. It feels too good," she murmured softly before grabbing a pillow burying her face in it.

He wasn't satisfied with a half ass job, but since she was satisfied he guessed it was time to dive in. Standing to his feet, Jess rolled back onto the bed, making room for him to climb on. Penis still on hard, he opened her tight, warm and wet pussy up with his love pole, stroking slowly as their bodies embraced the low impact physical collisions.

Warm air filled the room and it was like the walls were hugging them. The more he stroked, the more her body welcomed him further inside. When Triple J grabbed a handful of her hair, she attempted to get away, knowing what time it was. Holding her head still, he licked the inside of her ear. Jessica's ear was one of her hot spots. He massaged her hot spot with circular waves from his tongue.

For a good while, they engaged in foreplay and had grown folks sex until Triple J turned it up. Beating across his chest with his bat waving like he was at home plate, he stood up onto the bed and beat some more.

"It's time for Willie D," he said, referring to his dick.

Willie D had that dick women couldn't stand because it was life changing, that good ole ghetto D women begged to take home, but he loved living with his mama. She's at work right now, so you gotta hurry up and pull up. Toot that ass up in the air, for that boom, bam, thank you ma'am, dick.

When Willie D came out, it was time to go ape shit.

Jessica knew the routine. She turned over, laying her face flat on the bed and arching her back perfectly as she pointed her ass to the ceiling. She spread her ass cheeks wide and got that big ole booty smacked with the palm of his hand.

Pow!

She jerked, reacting to the slap. Triple J grabbed the same oil she used coming out the bathroom and began pouring it all over her ass. Sliding back into her warm hole, he wasted no time beating her guts up from the doggy style position. Full, long, and hard-core back shots he gave to her, making her cum multiple times.

Going hard, he went ape shit until the second round of explosions that blasted off and raced heavier inside of her vagina. Hands raised high, he pumped them up and down like he'd won a heavyweight boxing match.

Shit Just Got Real.

---

2

*F*eeling fresh and clean as they climbed out of the shower together, Jessica and Triple J dried off with the same towel. They walked back to the room wearing bathrobes, but Jess dropped hers and climbed in bed wearing nothing but her birthday suit.

Hanging on to each other's hand, Triple J tried to make the best of their time together, being that his freedom was not promised in the future. He still hadn't told Jess about the phone call from his pop as he thought about how to do it.

Surfing through the thoughts of his mind, he figured the best way to do it was like Nike said, *Just Do It.*

"Jessie," he called her name out softly. "You know I love you so much, but it's something I need to tell you."

Her eyes grew huge, as she looked at him anxiously.

"What do you have to tell me that's so difficult?" She asks with sass in her voice.

Reaching out, he grabbed both of her hands because what he had to tell her he knew she was going to take hard. He looked deep into her eyes as his chest began to heave up and down as he prepared for the worst.

"Tell me!" she screamed, eager to know, "You better not be cheating on me with some broke bitch," she continued.

Hurting inside, he began to speak in a low tone.

"Pop called earlier with bad news. He said homicide detectives surrounded the house because I have a warrant for murder. I don't know much about what's going on, but I might have to lay down for a while."

A dreadful expression covered her face and then sho'nuff the tears followed, raining heavily from her eyes. Triple J couldn't stand to see his wife cry and now this horrible reality had hit home. All he'd done was go hard in the streets to financially better life for his family. Little thought went into the pain and suffering they would feel once shit gets real.

What would life be like with them separated? he thought.

He and Jessica were inseparable best friends. Neither of them could live without the other. As the tears began to run heavily from her eyes, all he could do was try to stay strong. Holding her head in his chest, the weight became heavy. Tears burst from his eyes and ran down his face like the Katrina flood when the levees broke.

Some things you could never take back and becoming the famous Triple J was one of them James regretted. He wished God had let him meet her before he'd gotten so deep in the streets.

Maybe I could have went all the way legit, he thought to himself. Triple J's instinctive antennas went up and on alert as the feeling of danger approached.

They coming! I need to get back to Atlanta, he thought.

After telling Jessica about his hunch, he quickly contacted

the pilot, dialing from the room phone since their cell phones were destroyed.

"We need to get wheels up in fifteen minutes," he said into the phone, waking him from his sleep.

"Copy that," the pilot responded.

Jessica packed her bags quickly and they moved for the door. Before exiting, she grabbed her husband's arm.

"Death shall do us apart, through thick and thin. We in this for the long haul," she said, quoting their favorite song "Long Haul" by Alley Boy and Kevin Gates.

Triple J leaned in to get a kiss before that feeling of danger struck him again. This time it was much closer, weird like right outside the room door.

Taking no chances, he pulled his Glock out, checked the slide to make sure one was up top before he looked through the peephole. Nothing seemed out of the ordinary, but when he snatched open the door with his pistol ready to buss, a bright mussel flash blinded him. From the right side of the hallway, a .223 round whistled past his head before the loud boom followed.

Quickly leaning back into the room, he pushed Jessica to the floor as he took cover at the edge of the door. Before he turned out to get shit popping, multiple male voices from the hallway screamed.

"Federal Agents! Put your gun down!"

As he turned to peek his head out, another shot came quickly missing for the second time. Men dressed in military grade tactical gear filled the hallway with their weapons pointed head level outside their room.

"Let me see your fucking hands! Let me see your hands!" they then yelled.

Triple J slid his strap back, getting it to Jessica quickly so she could tuck it away.

"I'm coming out," he said, stepping out with his hands raised.

"Get the fuck on the ground," multiple voices yelled. "Get down now! Get down!"

As he turned into the hallway and knelt on the floor to surrender, one of the officers grabbed his arm and twisted it, slamming him hard to the floor.

"A man, what the fuck? I'm not resisting," Triple J said to him.

Several of them then jumped onto his back, pressing their weight down and holding him against the floor.

"What is your name? What's your fucking name boy?" one of them yelled.

"Johnson. James Johnson Junior," Triple J replied, hoping to ease some of the tension on his back, but it didn't.

"I can't breathe with you on my neck," Triple J struggled to say in between short breaths.

"If you talking, you can breathe," one of them replied.

"I can't, sir. It's hard. Please let me stand up. I can't breathe."

"Do we have a positive I.D.?" one of them asked.

"Yes, Commander," another replied.

"Mr. James Johnson, Junior, you're being arrested for outstanding warrants out of Atlanta, Georgia for conspiracy to commit murder. You have the right to remain silent. Anything you say can and will be used against you."

As his rights were being read, all he could think was, *Damn, shit just got real.*

Breaking News

Texas authorities report that within the last hour, wanted fugitive James "Triple J" Johnson, Junior was apprehended by Federal U.S. Marshals after a forty-five-minute standoff with SWAT.

Sources say that Mr. Johnson was found hiding in the tub of his expensive 5-Star hideaway hotel suite who gave the Marshals a struggle while being taken into custody.

Not much information is being given to the press at this time, but sources on the scene claimed to have heard several gunshots coming from inside the room. Federal Investigators have been sighted entering the location after Triple J's arrest and are supposedly investigating the Marshals involved shooting at the time.

I contacted the FBI's field office, but no one is answering questions as the investigation continues.

Stay tuned for more reports.

I'm Melissa Waters and this is Atlanta's number one news station WISN 2, the first to get the news and deliver it to you."

3

This whole situation is some Grade A bull shit. The only good thing for Triple J right now was the U.S. Marshals SUV's air conditioner.

He laid his head back on the head rest trying to find a place to relax, but the uncomfortable handcuffs around his wrist made it difficult to fit his back in the cushions of the seat. As the Marshals stripped out of their gear, Triple J became more agitated listening to them talk that police ass shit.

"I didn't have a clear shot. I could have taken him," one said.

"Yeah, you should have so I could get his fine ass wife. Did y'all see that bitch ass?" another one asked.

For thirty plus minutes, Triple J sat and listened to all their bull shit cop talk, before they finally decided to climb in.

As they were pulling away, he saw a woman seated in the passenger seat of the truck on the side of them. She looked familiar, but he couldn't really make her out ~~good~~ from behind the tint.

Cuffed and uncomfortable, Triple J closed his eyes to hide the anger he had for these folks. Taking deep inhales and slow exhales of air, he slowed his heart rate and cleared his thoughts.

Falling into a relaxed state, he opened his eyes as they broke onto an airport tarmac. Outside of their truck was a large 747 commercial aircraft parked with its passenger doors opened and a long set of stairs that ran down from it.

Two plain-clothes guys, one wearing a small bag over his shoulder, stepped off the plane and walked to their truck. He and the driver talked for a few seconds outside the truck then took Triple J out.

The Marshal standing next to him removed a pair of black and silver scissors off his duty belt and clipped the plastic cuffs one hand at a time. Relieved of the uncomfortable cuffs, he rubbed his wrist, twisting his hand back and forth around them, hoping to ease some of the pain the fisticuffs had caused.

"Mr. Johnson, I'm U.S. Marshal David Miles and this is my partner, U.S. Marshal Timothy Humphrey," the black guy said as he introduced himself in an up north accent. He nodded his head to the right side towards the tall white guy that stood next to him as he continued in a settled tone.

"I read your transport report and see you are a luxurious man. You've traveled to several counties on your private jet and even have your own pilot. Now, I couldn't get you a special flight like that, but I did arrange first class seating for you on this one," he said, turning towards the commercial aircraft. "By no means do we wish to make this any more uncomfortable than it already is for you, so please follow our commands and this will be the best flight you've been on at the expense of the United States Government. We're going to leave your hands free out of respect for who you are. Please don't make any crazy moves and everything will be okay. You understand what I'm saying."

"Yes," he answered him, while nodding his head up and down.

Marshal Miles turned and led the way back to the plane. Triple J trailed with Marshal Humphrey close behind.

"Fucking birdies. Who do they think they are?" one of the Marshals said as they were walking off. Marshal Miles heard them and laughed, never looking back to see which one it was.

No one but the flight staff was on board when they climbed on. And greeting them at the door smiling cheerfully, was a beautiful brown skinned woman with nice dreaded hair. She had them styled to the back braided neatly to her head. She showed them their first-class seats and took off behind the curtain near the captain's cabin.

In many ways, Triple J's was thankful for the separation from the crowds of passengers in business class and coach. It was a tough situation for him, but better than being cuffed and cooped up in that truck driving all the way back to Georgia.

While they sat there, he wondered how Jess was dealing with this. She probably was in full motion right now on the jet back to Atlanta.

Marshal Miles and Humphrey flipped through their phones while they waited for the plan to finish boarding. A small group of college age girls sat near them and one was sho'nuff eye candy. She waved at Triple J, blushing at the unchained prisoner.

"What's hannin'? What's y'all name?" he asked, speaking in his southern slang.

"Hey, I'm Rebecca and these are my friends, Ashley and Amanda," she said.

"Okay, I'm James but everyone calls me Triple J. Where y'all headed to?"

"The ATL," the trio sang in unison.

"First time?"

"Yeah, we're dancers and heard that's where the money at," Rebecca answered him.

"Yeah, most definitely. Y'all look like some intelligent woman and I don't want you to go astray. Atlanta Strip Clubs are cutthroat for new girls looking to make some money. When y'all touch down, go check out Farm Girls Strip Club and holla at Mello DS. Tell him Triple J sent you."

"Are you the Triple J Wild Child Wolf he talks about in the song?"

"Yeah that's me," Triple J replied humbly.

"Can we have a picture please?" Amanda asked, pulling out her phone.

"Sorry, no pictures today, ladies," Marshal Humphrey said, standing up in between them and Triple J.

"Excuse me! Mr. Triple J your security is rude," Rebecca said as she attempted to look around Humphrey.

"He's not really my security and I apologize," Triple J said as Humphrey flashed his U.S. Marshals shield.

"Oh, I'm sorry, sir," Rebecca replied in a bit of shock.

Saved by the plane starting up, the pilot's voice came over the intercom.

"Attention, passengers. This is your captain speaking. I

would like to welcome you aboard to flight AF22.12 headed for Airport ATL. Please find your seats and fasten your seat belts as this flight prepares for takeoff. Thank you for joining us and please stay seated until the seat belt sign is turned off. Again, this is your captain, chief pilot of flight AF22.12 headed for the great ATL."

Triple J stared out of the window as the pilot steered to the runway. With an unknowing future, he gathered as many good memories as he could before going to jail.

Alongside the plane, yellow and white lights blinked through the darkened night, capturing his attention. As soon as they changed over to green, the plane picked up its speed and off into the midnight skies they went. Turbulence was heavy once they were into the sky, but the pilot got a hold of things quickly and it was off to a smooth sail.

"Would you like something to drink?" the beautiful female flight attendant asked, standing with her serving cart in the aisle.

Her eyes are centered on Triple J and his eyes were locked on her too.

Oh my God! She's a beauty, he thinks to himself.

She was a 5'4" dark and lovely cutie pie. She was serving alcoholic beverages but before he even took a drink, he was already drunk off her curvy hips. She was busting literally, so much so that she'd stretched the stitching on her skirt. Caught up in her anointing, Triple J just stared at her, forgetting to order.

"Would you like something to drink?" she asked for a second time in a beautiful, melodic singing voice.

Since the Marshal intervened with him taking a picture, he looked over at Humphrey and then Miles for confirmation. Both of the Marshals asked for water, but Miles ordered him a glass of Hennessy on light rocks.

That's a little strange, Triple J thought. The Marshals weren't drinking but gave him free will to. It just doesn't seem right.

Triple J knew he had to be on point with these guys after watching several murder investigations on TV. These guys were federal agents and had the best of training in the United States.

These investigators playing all types of games. Keep your ears open and your mouth closed. Loose lips sink ships, he told himself.

The beautiful black Barbie continued her work after she fixed their beverages. As she maneuvered down the aisle, for some reason, she couldn't keep her eyes off Triple J.

"It looks like somebody has a crush," Marshal Miles said, instigating the attraction.

"Oh really," Humphrey replied, playing dumb like he doesn't see it.

"Yes, sir. She can't resist him. Look at her. She keeps looking back."

"Mr. Johnson, I didn't take you for being afraid of women," Marshal Miles said, double nudging Triple J's arm with his elbow. "I know if I was going to jail, I wouldn't wanna go without getting me some before I went in," he continued. trying to hype him up.

Triple J ignored them because he never needed any jumper cables to start up the whip, so he figured why should he use them now. He remembered he is the King of the Apes, Mr. Ape Shit and he was trained to go on the mark.

Jessica had his heart, mind, body and soul. They agreed if

there was ever any fresh meat, they were going to do her together.

The Marshals continued with the small talk and Triple J silently listened. He had very little conversation for the pigs. Even though he sipped a little drink and became settled, he was super focused.

Marshal Miles then began to speak about himself and his upbringing in Paterson, New Jersey. The community where he was from was like many other urban communities. He claimed to once have been a part of a neighborhood clique called PSP, the Paterson Street Posse. When his best friend was shipped upstate with life plus thirty years in their senior year of high school, for murder, he folded his flag and signed up for the military.

Running away from his life of crime, he began his twenty-year military career at the age of seventeen and retired at thirty-seven with an honorable discharge.

"So, tell us about you, Triple J," Marshal Miles said after he finished.

"Huh?" he replied, shaking his head as he played like he hadn't been listening, "Oh yeah! Everything's good," he continued, pretending to be dumbfounded.

Their strategy was weak and Triple J recognized it off the dribble. Marshal Miles came up with this incredible hood story so that he could get some information from Triple J making it seem like he owed the Marshal a story, as well.

Triple J knew he had been arrested for conspiracy to commit a murder and anything he said could and would be used against him. He continued the dumb role because if he said the wrong thing, he would be slammed like crushed rocks.

Rolling up the aisle again, serving food trays, his crush

flight attendant returned. Even though they didn't order food, she still laid a neatly prepared meal before them.

It was grilled chicken with mushroom sauce and two-baked potatoes that sat on the main dish. Strawberry ice cream with crushed nuts sprinkled across the top sat on the side.

Not really hungry, but forcing himself to eat, Triple J dove in with his plastic spork, digging off in the grilled chicken first. From all the jailhouse stories he'd heard about the food, he took his time and chewed his food well, knowing this very well could be his last free world meal.

With a huge blush spreading across her face, the attendant returned with liquid refills.

"Was it good?" she asked. "Can I get you something else?" she continued with her eyes locked on Triple J.

"Yes, ma'am! Surprisingly, it really was good," Triple J said. "Thank you for serving me. I appreciate it. I don't think I have room for anything extra, but I do need to use the restroom."

"Yes, King. Just follow me," she said pleasantly.

Humphrey stood to let Triple J out into the aisle, he then began to follow them, until Marshal Miles called him back.

"Humphrey, let him go. He's just going to make a head call," Miles said.

He had no idea what he was referring to when he said "Head call" as Triple continued to the restroom. Down the aisle, they reached the front of the plane and stepped behind a burgundy curtain. He wasn't expecting to be taken to the staff restroom and right now he doesn't care.

Rushing quickly inside, he didn't even think to lock the door behind himself.

As soon as the toilet flushed, he was bombarded by the door that slammed against his back.

"I can't take this no more. I know you want me," the flight attendant said as she slid into the tight toilet room.

Chopping against her forearm, he blocked her hand from grabbing his crotch as she continued to charge forward.

"You gone give me this dick," she said.

Damn, Shit Just Got Real.

4

*W*restling his outstretched hands against her shoulders, the flight attendant put up a physical fight to get to him.

"What the hell is your problem?" Triple J asked as she continued to charge forward with her eyes closed. "I'm married, Miss Lady," he yelled at her.

"I'm deaf. I can't hear none of that bull shit," she responded sarcastically.

Turning her butt towards him, she folded at the waist and pressed her soft and plump ass against his crotch.

Quickly lifting up her skirt, she exposed her pretty and perfectly round booty buns. Jiggling them around in her purple thong panties, Triple J looked down and was amazed.

"Wow! This is crazy. I'm being raped by a bad bitch," he said aloud with his head facing the restroom roof. Slick enjoying her persistence to have him, he lessened his fight to push her off.

Knowing he was married, and his wife was accepting of them having another woman, he wondered, *How the story was supposed to be told when he got to jail. I had sexy black cutie pie, dumb thick, flight attendant raping me on the plane when I was coming to jail, but I fought her off?*

The only person that could tell that story was a guy solely into men.

"I'm married, Miss Lady," he said again but she didn't acknowledge anything he was saying like she was really deaf.

Turning to face him, she dropped to her knees and quickly snatched his penis out like a lady ninja swift and quick.

"Aye! Hold the fuck up! What's wrong with you?" he yelled at her, but she just continued to fight like a female MMA fighter, getting him to submit with a smile on her face.

Leaning forward to wrap her lips around his pole, Triple J tried to pull away in the tight space. She took him in her mouth, wrapping her glossy lips around his pole.

Sluurrp. She sucked in with her tongue sticking out of her mouth.

"I told you I'm married, ma'am," he said, weakened by the joys of her lips.

"Mmmhmm, I know," she replied with her mouth full.

"Well, get off." She continued to suck him off, slurping and bobbing her head up and down.

Damn, I didn't know getting rape would feel so good, he thought to himself. *I'm kind of enjoying this crazy woman. She's going in like she's competing in the Dick Sucking Olympics.*

Pausing to stand to her feet, she grabbed a hold of him and stroked her hand down his shaft. Pulling him with her to the tiny sink, she climbed backwards and threw her legs high and wide.

As he slid inside of her, she gasped for air while scratching her nails across his back. Ripping the skin, she sent excruciating pain down his spine, but he took it as a gear changer.

Pounding hard in her little tight box, she screamed from both the punishing and pleasuring. Small nibbles against the top of her ear really drove her crazy.

"Agh!" she screamed, still tearing away at his back.

Body fluids erupted from her vagina back-to-back and ran like water down his leg. Flying through the night sky having sex on a plane was not on the bucket list for the married man, but he was sure enjoying it. Once again, the Pimp God has fucked with Pimping.

Together their eruptions happened and both bodies locked at the same time. Triple J tried pulling out, but lost his footing from her wetness, falling deeper inside her vagina walls. Regret immediately started to race through his mind as he slid up his pants.

Damn, I hope she doesn't get pregnant. That's gone fuck up my marriage, he thought to himself.

Before exiting the restroom, she leaned in for a kiss, but he immediately got upset and pushed her away.

"Hell naw, bitch. You already raped me."

"And, you liked it," she replied, rolling her neck with her hand on her hip like an upset female teenager.

Hurrying back to his seat, he got there quickly as he fled from the crazy woman.

"You have sweat on your forehead," Marshal Miles said.

"Yeah, constipation. I had to take a shit," Triple J answered.

"We both know you weren't taking a shit," Humphrey said firmly and direct in his interrogation voice. "What I wanna know is, did you eat the ass?"

"What kind of crazy freaky shit is this man on?" Triple J

asked himself. "What kind of question is that? I'm black and packing. Real men don't eat ass," he replied aggressively.

"Calm down, Mr. Johnson. He's just joking," Marshal Miles said, interjecting. "Tell me this though. Did you get the pussy?" he asked humbly, playing that good cop bad cop role.

Not answering him verbally and trying to keep his poker face, Triple J gave himself away with his smile.

"Yeah, he got it. Look, it's all over his face. Now pay me," Miles said.

Humphrey reached into his back pocket and removed his wallet. Thumbing through the bills, he gave Marshal Miles a crispy twenty-dollar bill.

Over the intercom, the pilot interrupted them again. The seat belt light came on and they buckled up.

"Attention, passengers. Please fasten your seatbelt as we begin to descend into Airport ATL."

For Triple J, things were bittersweet. Although his tanks were empty and he was sexually satisfied, it was time to face reality.

The other passengers exited the plane before them and once they got the all clear from the flight staff, Miles and Humphrey got him up to leave. Triple J's new flight attendant baby mama blushed at them as they stepped off. She waved good-bye their entire way up the ramp. Waiting for them at the top of the exit ramp, deep in numbers were members of the Atlanta City Police.

Miles and Humphrey knew they would be here, but Triple J was left in shock.

"You're gonna be alright, Mr. Johnson," Marshal Miles whispered over Triple J's shoulder. "Make sure you read Psalms 91 and 27 every day. God has great plans for your life. He's going to use you for his will."

While he stared in shock, several officers surrounded him and grabbed a hold to his arms.

"Put your hands behind your back, Mr. Johnson. You're under arrest."

A camera flash blinded Triple J as the officer cuffed him. Right then Triple J knew, Shit Just Got Real.

5

---

*T*he arrest of Triple J had become a big deal around the whole city of Atlanta . Atlanta's City Police were blocking the streets like the presidential motorcade came through, blue lights and sirens blaring in every direction. Triple J began to realize this shit was real and not some TV prank. As they were riding, he recognized the highest-ranking policeman in the city was sitting in the passenger seat of the same SUV as him.

*"Why would Chief Robinson be riding with me,"*he asked himself.

Many questions raced through his mind and as the motorcade slowed down near the Public Safety Headquarters, he learned the answer to them. He was the talk of the town, large crowds of multiracial pedestrians gathered on both sides of Peachtree Street, holding handmade signs along the sidewalk.

"Really? All of this is for me," Triple J asked himself as he looked around.

Two signs, "Free Triple J" and "Free the Real Ones, Keep the Fakes", were displayed that he was able to read.

The closer they got to the headquarters, news vans and groups of elderly white women sat in collapsible chairs, holding their own unfriendly signs, "Make Atlanta Great Again" and "Thank You, APD. GET THEM OFF OUR STREETS.".

"If that ain't about a bitch," he said aloud, voicing his reaction.

Their signs spoke out on how a lot of people felt in so many words, "Every black man's guilty until proven innocent."

Heavy chatter went out over the radio as they pulled into the complex.

Chief Robinson gave orders over his ~~Apple~~ iPhone to allow the cameras into the facility's parking area.

As the SUV came to a halt, crowds of cameras and microphones raced ahead, quickly surrounding the truck. Several officers struggled to get in between them and the truck. Some even had to forcefully push the reporters back just to get Triple J out. Chief Robinson was the first to grab a hold of Triple J's arm, escorting him up the stairs to the main entrance.

"Mr. Johnson? Mr. Johnson? Is it really true you ordered the murder of Clarence Coleman?" a popular reporter from the local news asked, holding a mic out to his face as they walked inside.

Triple J knew he was going to be on TV and with all this love and community support outside, he answered the reporter's question with his million-dollar smile on.

"Well sir, it's like this. I'm a hard-working taxpaying man that's brought many jobs to the city. I'm not in business with any mercenaries and I've never ordered anyone to murder anyone. I just wanna say Poppa, I love ya. ANW, hold it down."

Chief Robinson seemed to be upset with the self-made millionaire, the way he snatched Triple J by the arm. As they were walking into the building, he then forcefully pushed the mogul through the ajar glass door.

Cameras continued behind them inside, echoing questions from reports from over the walls of the lobby. Behind the screening area, the police chief relinquished Triple J over to one of the lobby officers.

"Take this filth upstairs," Chief Robinson spat, referring to Triple J.

"Filth?"

"Yeah, your filth!" he continued as he wailed off words in the soon to be billionaire's face. Never had he been called filth.

The tone in the chief's voice let Triple J know this wasn't about who was right or who was wrong, this was personal. Silent after the chief's negative reference to him, Triple J continued into the elevator with the team of officers escorting him.

The Atlanta's Major Crimes Division & Homicide sign is what they saw when they stepped off the elevator onto the third floor. Triple J was escorted through a pair of magnetic locked wooden double doors and the first person he saw was his attorney, Torris J.,Esquire thumbing through his phone.

Torris J., Esquire also known as T.J., the legal guru, was one of the best criminal defense attorneys and the greatest the State Bar of Georgia had seen in many years.

He had a 98% trial victory rate and last year received the most prestigious award from the Black Lawyers of America for a high-profile appeal he had won in Fulton County's Appellate Court. He was hands down the best attorney anyone could hire, especially at a time like this.

"May I have a place to speak privately to my client?" TJ asked the police captain seated at a desk across from him.

"Yes, sir. Sargent Davis, please take Mr. Johnson into the attorney's conference room," the Captain instructed him.

As they were walking down the hallway, they passed several private rooms. Many of them had sliding bolts outside of them.

T.J. followed them closely with his black leather briefcase in hand. His head was held high like he's carrying a million bucks inside.

Can you say confident?

The investigators knew he was one of the best to ever come in the game and many of them were intimidated by the educated, black man. At the end of the hall, Triple J was first taken into an office-sized room with very little furniture— one clear table desk and two chairs, one on each side. T.J. was asked to wait outside while the Sargent uncuffed Triple J and shackled him around both ankles to the floor.

"Good Morning, Mr. Johnson. First, let me ask you, are you injured in any way?" TJ asked him as soon as the officers left out and closed the door.

"Naw! Nothing major."

"Okay, good. I was worried sick about you when your wife called and informed me you were shot at during the arrest. I've been down here talking to every bigwig since first thing this morning."

"No one ever contacted me and gave us the option to do this thing safely. When I found out about the warrant, you were already taken into custody."

"That's cool, I had a heads up."

"Good. Well, right now they're telling me very little. I'm just getting a copy of the warrant and affidavit. You were wanted for murder conspiracy and felony murder. So far from what I've seen, they don't have much. I'm making calls all over Georgia right now on your behalf and we should have a bond within the next two weeks.

"You're going to Fulton jail when you leave here. Be safe and don't talk to anyone about your case. Stay out the way and I'll get you out of there as soon as possible."

"The detectives wanna get a statement from you and ask a few questions. I just had to see you before I tell them we're declining to cooperate."

The attorney knew that if he asked Triple J what he wanted to do, it wouldn't be any talk. No statement is the best statement, the OGs always told him growing up. Before leaving to prepare Triple J's defense strategies, T.J. dapped his client up, and left him with several instructions.

"You're going to jail around everybody that wants to get out. Please don't talk to anyone about your case, selling you out is a freedom ticket. Things are going to be rough in there. Stay to yourself, keep your mouth close, listen with your ears and you're going to be alright."

As he was talking, Triple J knew things were going to be rough for him on the inside because everybody and their mama knew him. It wouldn't be simple to stay under the radar. Things weren't anything like what he imagined.

Shit Just Got Real.

The Press Conference

43

Several local news teams waited in the police briefing area that had been transformed into a pressroom.

On a slightly elevated platform, several investigators and Atlanta City Police white shirts marched out with Chief Robinson and stood behind a glass framed podium with ACP's insignia on the front. First to the mic was the chief.

"Good morning and thank you all, citizens of the community and members of the media, for coming out today witnessing the historic arrest of Atlanta's Most Wanted individual, James "Triple J" Johnson, Junior. First I'm going to bring veteran Detective Jim O'Connor to the podium to deliver the great news to everyone. Everyone please give him a warm round of applause."

Several people in the crowd stood and clapped as the detective approached the mic.

"Thank you, Chief Robinson, for the astounding introduction, but the applause really belongs to you," he said, looking over at the chief. "Without your leadership, the ACP would be just another department and not the number one department in the southeast. First, I wanna thank you all for coming to today's capture celebration for Atlanta's Most Wanted individual. On Saturday, September 28th, 2013, James "Triple J" Johnson, Junior ordered several members of his ANW crime family to carry out the vicious slaughtering of Clearance "Lil Cece" Coleman a father of three.

Witnesses stated four unidentified males wearing ski-masks and hoodies and bearing high powered rifles stood in front of Mr. Coleman like a firing squad, and shot him repeatedly. When Mr. Colman's body was found, he was tied to a telephone pole and his body was riddled with bullets. For two plus years, we were left without much to follow up on in Mr. Coleman's case. Things were cold until an anonymous tip came into our office. The caller gave specific details that were not released to the public and identified four members of the ANW crime organization as the perpetrators.

Our team of investigators followed up on those leads and the four perps were arrested and charged last year. Today we're celebrating the ring leader's capture. Cell phone records show Mr. Johnson placed multiple calls from his cellular phone to one of the shooters on the scene before and after the shots were reported.

A confidential informant has come forward corroborating the cell phone's evidence with a third-party confession from Mr. Johnson of what happened on the night of the murder. A warrant was obtained for Mr. Johnson and he's been charged with conspiracy and felony murder. This investigation is ongoing and if you have any information please call crime catchers at 404-ATL-TIPS. Again, the number is 404-ATL-T.I.P.S. Thank you."

6

_F_or thirty plus years, the crime boss Triple J, had been skating around the police, avoiding the jail cell. As he sat and waited, stories he had heard about his future residence ran through his mind.

"Whatever you do, make sure you watch out for Big Bubble. He hangs around the shower, looking for fresh meat to drop the soap," his Uncle Flash used to say, scaring him when he was growing up. Several times he ran in the room on Lil James, while he was asleep, scaring him awake.

"What you gone do fuck or fight?" his uncle used to ask him.

It wasn't no talking. The young Triple J just started swinging, catching him slap dead on the nose. After several hours of wild thoughts, he was awakened by Sargent Aldridge, unlatching the lock to the room he was waiting in.

"Let's go, Johnson," he said as he stepped inside.

Triple J was dressed down in his exclusive pieces of jewelry for his transport to jail. Waist chains and ankle cuffs were placed on him restricting his movement to very minimum.

This is so belittling, he thought to himself. *I'm literally a slave locked in balls and chains.*

As they walked out into the hallway, Triple J saw there was a group of additional officers positioned to follow them out the door.

Entering the elevator, Triple J found himself stuffed toward the rear of it. He was forced into the corners, against the wall with the group of eight piled up behind him. Stepping off the elevator, they ran right back into the crowd of ready reporters. Triple J was oblivious to the press conference that went on while he was upstairs waiting and was again surprised when they reached the bottom of the elevator.

"Is it true what these detectives are saying? Did you have Clarence 'Little Cece' Coleman killed?" one reporter asked.

"Will the courts find you guilty?" another one screamed.

Before T.J. left, he instructed Triple J not to say a word to the media.

"I'll handle the news. You just be calm and ignore the reports," he said.

The crowds grew heavier outside of headquarters and the police struggled to keep control. Many of the protesters were hype and loud in support of Triple J, the powers that be were afraid a riot would break out as they sung the ANW Anthem.

"Ape shit, Ape shit, Ape shit and Wolves, Ape shit and Wolves. Ape shit, Ape shit, Ape shit and Wolves, Ape shit and Wolves."

"That's right, ANW. This our city," Triple J said in a low tone to the crowd.

When the officers finally got the city's most favored

criminal into the transporting truck, everyone was on high alert as they pulled out into larger crowds of Triple J's supporters. The blue lights were flashing, and sirens were blaring as the crowds ignited and turned up.

Several people stormed out into the street, blocking the caravan from moving forward surrounding the truck Triple J was riding in.

"They doing all this for me?" he asked himself as he looked out the windows.

Several of them let it be known they were not with the cops. They held "Free Triple J" support signs, pumping them up and down. When the foot officers stormed out of the station with shields and batons, the protesters cleared the streets quickly, running from the riot squad. Triple J's police caravan immediately took off when the roads opened enough for them to go.

Reaching speeds of ninety plus miles an hour, they sped down Northside Drive, rushing him to the county jail. When the crowd of police vehicles slowed down, nervous chills shot across his body. He'd heard so many stories about Fulton Jail and now that he was there, he knew it was real. Surprisingly, this was his first time ever seeing the place.

Damn this bitch is huge, Triple J thought as he looked up at the jail from the back gate.

The transport SUV pulled into the driveway of the jail and the other police vehicles hung a left leaving Triple J and the two officers upfront to enter the compound alone. Clearing the guards' shack, the officer pulled around the long driveway, stopping at several slide gates before reaching a large sally port garage to the jail.

The truck stopped and the officer put the gear in park. Down came the garage door closing behind them, lowering from a thirty-foot ceiling. Triple J was taken from the back seat and was more nervous than ever. The loud echo from the door closing startled him as he walked inside.

"Welcome to Fulton Jail. I know you think you're a tough guy, but they got some real killers in here. My advice for you is to not drop the soap. You know you're a pretty nigga," the young punk, Officer J. Williams, said as they approached the burnt orange sliding doors.

Triple J had a fire comeback for the young officer that was gone make him think long and hard before he used another gay joke, but he let him have that. He had serious issues to deal with. "Male Intake" was painted across the burnt orange door they were leading him to. It led them into a medium-sized square area with large windows on three sides of the room. Two large, statured black men, wearing green uniforms and black brimmed caps falling over their eyes, stood in the center of the floor at ease. When Triple J stepped inside, they pointed him towards a metal countertop connected to the cinder block wall.

"Take everything you have in your pockets out. Place them on the counter and when you're done, lay your hands flat on the counter in front of you," he said in a loud baritone voice. "And hurry yo' ass up to. I'm tired and I don't feel like being down here with this shit," he continued to say.

Reaching into his pocket and removing the content he had, Triple J did what he was told before he laid his hands flat.

"Is that everything, nigga? Because if something pokes me, I'm gone beat yo' ass."

"Yeah, that's it, sir," he replied respectfully.

"Yeah!" he screamed back at the crime boss. "Did you just yea me? First, let's get one thing clear, fuck nigga! This my jail. And I don't give a fuck who you were out there or who you 'pose to be in the streets, I run this shit. You gone respect me. It's yes sir! Do you understand me?" the bad breath officer screamed in his face.

"Yes sir," Triple J answered him nonchalantly, not really trying to trip with dude.

"Wham!" the green giant punched the crime boss hard in the abdomen, shoving his fist through his gut.

With nothing to break his fall, Triple J folded over holding his stomach when he fell to the floor.

"Zzzzz!" The green giant used a black taser to zap him repeatedly in the side, causing his body to jerk sporadically from the shock.

Grabbing hold of the officer's hand, Triple J managed to take the taser from him. A hard kick in the side, made him release the taser just as quick as he took it.

When Triple J turned in the direction of the kick, he saw ACP Officer J. Williams was the one that kicked him. Muscling up to his feet, the four officers used all of the strength they had to keep Triple J down.

"Stop resisting! Stop resisting!" they screamed as he continued to rise.

Several other officers responded to the radio call the booth officer made to get Triple J down.

"Stop resisting! Stop Resisting!" they continued to yell.

So many different bodies piled on top of Triple J's back, smashing him into the tiled floors. Many of the officers ran in swinging and punching, getting cheap blows while he was restrained. One of the officers pressed his knee into Triple J's neck, restricting his air intake. As he lay pressed into the floor, unable to breathe with tears built up in his eyes, he realized, Shit Just Got Real.

7

*S*ome people just didn't believe shit stank until it was a part of their wardrobe. The stunt these offi-cers pulled jumping on the ANW crime boss was pure suicidal and was equivalent to flipping over a trash truck. Shit was about to get real nasty for somebody's child.

As he laid across the floor, cuffed and unable to breathe, Triple J's blood boiled.

The Black Lives Matter Movement irritated Triple J at first. He thought that they were just a bunch of black folks crying and complaining. But now he understood why people were angrily protesting, blocking the streets, marching and screaming, "Black Lives Matter." The movement was impor-tant and Triple J realized that now. Cops were given too much power, and immunity to do what they wanted to do. Not in this case though, something had to be done.

As the pain subsided in Triple J's neck from the officer kneeling on him, Triple J remained on the floor. He lifted his head with tears flowing from his eyes and saw a tall black man standing over him. Wearing his creased and clean sheriff's uniform, Captain James stared down at the crime boss.

"Stand him up," he said to the officers holding Triple J down on the floor.

They lifted Triple J to his feet by his arms and stood him in front of Captain James. Face to face, they stared into each other's eyes, neither looking away. Captain James, however, was the first to look away, scanning the floor like he lost something.

"When they told me you were at the back gate, I came down to see you and this what you do? Scuff up my floors? My orderlies just waxed and buffed them."

Triple J looked at the Captain angrily. He was staring at him "like are you serious?"

"Man, this shit tile. Not marble, so miss me with that hoe shit. You come down here talking about a damn floor and my fucking side hurt," he snapped back.

Captain James laughed and walked off. This whole incident let Triple J know not to trust any of them. From the bottom to the top, they were all dirty, but everything happens for a reason. His shirt was stretched all out of whack from them mopping him across the nasty floor as Triple J stood in filth. Medical nurse from inside the jail came with a red duffle bag on her arm.

"Are you injured anywhere?" she asked Triple J, checking for injuries.

"Naw. No ma'am," he answered even though his arm was in excruciating pain.

"They're all working together against me," he said to himself. He didn't trust any of them, including the medical nurse. She continued to look him over, checking for any visible injuries. When she saw none, she smiled and walked away.

"Alright! He's fine, y'all."

Several of the jailers returned inside along with the ACP officers to sign Triple J in. The two green giants stayed with Triple J, taking him into a small padded cell to be strip-searched.

I hope they're not trying to turn me into a nutcase, Triple J thought to himself when they took him into the same cell they kept mental health patients.

"Take everything off," one of them said. "Your shirts, pants, boxers, shoes and socks. Hand each of them to me as you take it off."

Uncomfortable stripping for the two men, Triple J slowly began to take off his clothes, handing them his shirt first.

When the officer grabbed his shirt, he shook it rapidly, then squeezed it from top to bottom. He did the same with the rest of his clothes but paused at the boxers.

"Them too," the jailer told him. So uncomfortable stripping down to his birthday suit in front of the two men, Triple J complied, in hopes to hurry up and get it over with.

"Hold your arms out in front of you with your palms up," the green giant said to the bare-naked Triple J. "Now, turn your hands around with your fingers spread wide," he continued. "Open your mouth and lift up your tongue." Triple J continued to cooperate. "Spread your legs and lift up your nut sack. Turn around, squat and cough," the green giant said.

Triple J paused as he thought, *Hold up. What did he just say to me?*

He had already felt violated after being naked in front of two men who might fuck around with the rainbow crew. Now they wanted him to bend over in front of them. To him, that was not gone happen.

"He said turn around, squat and cough," the spectating green giant yelled. "Ain't nobody got time to play with you. Hurry up and get this shit over with."

Triple J hated everything about the strip search, but he complied with the squat and cough, not wanting to become a human punching bag for a second time in one day.

"Ough!" he coughed once while he squatted down and popped right back up.

"Cough again," the grenny said. "You might got something stuck up ya ass."

Triple J looked at him with rage in his eyes. "Da fuck you say to me, duck ass pig? You got me fucked up if you ever think anything going in my ass. Matter of fact, give me my shit before I go ape shit in this motherfucka," he said, finally frustrated with them. The green jailer threw his clothes on the floor and kicked them at him.

"Here, put this shit on," he said, demanding him to get dressed.

Triple J saw they were trying to aggravate him, so he moved quickly to get dressed, climbing into his boxers and then his pants. With only one leg in his pants, the green giant that punched him tried to sneak him again. But this time, Triple J was ready as he rushed him into the wall. Reacting quickly to the green uniform officer trying to rush him, Triple J dropped down and pivoted, punching him in the knee three rapid times, which reversed the greenies intentions to throw him into the wall. Before Triple J could bash him in the head, his partner grabbed his arm quickly.

"Y'all bitch niggas gone stop playing with me," he said as the officer twisted his hand behind his back. Sandwiched in between the two, Triple J held the sneaky officer against the wall.

"You gone have a serious problem if—if you don't let me go," he said, choking up on his words.

Triple J knew he could take them both right now and neither would have a chance to get off a blow on him. Instead of giving them a second round, he let the greenie go but later regretted it.

"You must want that real smoke?" the one Triple J had pinned against the wall asked.

"Fuck nigga! I am the mothafucking smoke," he spat back with authority. "I'm the fire, smoke and rain. I promise on everything you can count your last days."

The one thing that never lied were the eyes. The green giant heard and saw in his eyes that Triple J was not playing and released him.

"You right," he said. "I'm gone let you put ya clothes on. I don't want you calling PREA on me," he said, trying not to show any fear.

"I don't know who the fuck, or what the fuck that is. But I can promise you that you don't have to worry about them," he spat back at the officer as he released his arm.

PREA was the Prison Rape Elimination Act. It was put in place to protect prisoners from sexual assault and sexual harassment by prisoners and staff members. For the green team member to mention something like that, Triple J knew he'd been accused before for something similar. Little did they know, Triple J was a big fish for real and the call he was going to make was one that would end their lives. They had no idea that,

Shit Just Got Real.

8

---

*A*fter multiple altercations with the jail's staff, Triple J exhaled a sigh of relief now that he was finally inside. Stopping at the officer's desk first, he put all of his pocket property and jewelry into a small evidence bag. The Marshals in Texas allowed him to give Jess most of it, but he still had on his watch and triple cross necklace. The couple hundred dollars he had in his pocket, the deputy told him to hold onto it.

"Before you go upstairs, you're gone put your money in the cash machine. It'll be on your books for commissary," the female deputy said.

Even though he had been cleared by medical once already for injuries, he still had to see them again. Taken to the nurses' station by the same green team jailers, Triple J walked through the thirteen-foot-tall door that had Medical Intake painted across it. Two female nurses sat at separate desks, their focus was locked in on their computers.

"Step on the scale so I can get your weight, please," one said as she rose from her seat, pointing Triple J to the right of the room. Walking over to the gray digital scale with a reader that came up to his chest, Triple J stepped up with his head held high.

"Okay you can step off. 185," she said once the digital scale finished calculating.

In blue ink, she recorded his weight on the back of her left gloved hand.

"And how tall are you?"

"Five eleven," he answered.

She recorded that also on her gloved hand before removing her lab coat, hanging it on the back of her chair. *Why did she do that*, he wondered to himself.

Blessed and highly favored, Triple J watched her assets dribble up and down as she moved quickly around the nurses' station. Directing him to her desk, Triple J took a seat in the chair on the left corner facing her. The green team jailers walked away, leaving him inside.

"How you doing today, Mr. Johnson?" the nurse asked in a beautiful soprano voice tone. "Are you nervous or something? You keep looking around like it's your first time."

"Yes, first time in the Georgia system," he answered.

"Oh, you're from a different state?"

"Naw, Atlanta born and raised in Grant Park Community."

"Oh, okay. It was another guy here earlier from Grant Park. He has a gorilla tattoo under his right eye. He was telling me it represented something called ANW. Apes and something I remember him saying because of the tattoo. Where else have you been locked up? You don't look like the type to get in trouble."

"Texas. And you're right, this not my forte," Triple J replied professionally.

"How was it there?"

"I can't tell you. I wasn't there long, but it's no place I ever wanna be arrested again," he said, shaking his head from left to right.

"Okay, Mr. Johnson. I need you to sign this medical consent form. It gives us permission to treat you in the event that you need medical attention."

"Ok," he said, grabbing the black pen attached to her desk.

One thing Triple J learned being in business was to read everything before you signed. Taking his time to read carefully, Triple J looked at every line and all words that might be hidden inside the consent form, even though she tried to rush him through it.

"I had to make sure I wasn't giving consent to cut my head off," he told her before signing.

"You don't think I'll do you like that would you?"

"You don't know what you'll do for some money."

"And what's that supposed to mean?"

"Think about it," he told her with a flirtatious blush.

"Alright, Mr. Johnson. Time to get back to the money," she said, winking at him, "I have a few questions for you. They are all confidential and will be handled with care in accordance with state medical privacy and protection laws. I'm not allowed to give any of this information to anyone without a court order or a medical records release form signed by you."

"Okay," Triple J answered.

"Answer these to the best of your ability. Do you have any health problems that you know of?"

"No."

"Are you on any medications prescribed by a doctor?"

"No."

"Have you had any surgeries?"

"No."

"Have you ever been diagnosed with any mental health disorders by a mental health professional?"

"No."

"Are you suicidal or homicidal in any way at this time?"

Triple J paused before he answered, thinking about the police that jumped on him.

"No!" he said angrily when the nurse looked up at him.

"You paused, Mr. Johnson. Is everything okay?" she asked.

"Yeah, it's all good!" he answered with a demonic look in his eyes.

"Okay, Mr. Johnson. I'm going to take your word. Are you currently under the influence of marijuana, meth, cocaine, heroin, molly, PCP, or any other street drug at this time?"

"No."

"Okay! Last one on this part. I can answer the rest of these when you leave. Please don't get offended, but I have to ask," she said, holding up her hand as if she was surrendering, "Your sexual preference? Women only, men only, or both?"

"Why the hell you gone ask me something like that? Woman only," Triple J said, snapping.

"I told you not to get offended. Look, the question is on here," she said, turning the computer screen towards him. "I been working down here a year now and you'd be surprised if you knew how many people come in and admit they like men only or both. The ones that say they like women only come in clean, go upstairs and back to medical with crouch breakouts. They be the toughest ones, trying to get mad at us because they went up there and contracted HIV. Ooh! While we're talking about it, let me go and give you your HIV test while you're down here. It will be a really quick small finger prick and you'll have the results in minutes."

"Okay, baby girl. And you don't have to worry about me coming back with crotch itch."

"You better not," she said. "While we're waiting for that to finish, I'm gonna give you your TB test. It's a real quick stick on top of the skin. Just to make sure you don't have tuberculosis."

"Tuberculosis! What's that?"

"A bacterial disease that affects your lungs. It causes severe coughs and fever. It's highly contagious and we have to check everyone for it when they first come in."

"Okay."

She opened the small plastic pack and grabbed Triple J's index finger. Giving it a small prick, she squeezed the tip of the finger, pushing the blood up and dumping it on a small white tray from the HIV test kit. With an orange and clear needle, she drew a clear liquid from a small glass bulb and shot it into Triple J's right forearm.

"That's your TB test. Somebody from medical will be here to check it in two days. While we wait for your HIV results to come back, I'm going to check your blood pressure so you can get on your way," she said. "You look tired."

"I'm in no rush. Take your time," Triple J replied.

As she wrapped the blood pressure cuff around his arm, thoughts of Jessica immediately came to his mind.

Damn, I miss my Jessie Pooh already, he thought to himself.

The machine beeped and the blood pressure cuffed loosened.

"Oh, Mr. Johnson. Your blood pressure is high. Are you on blood pressure medication?" she asked.

"No, do I need to be?"

"Well, your blood pressure is high, but that can come from a little stress. You know this being your first time," she said, winking her eye. "But I think you'll be fine once you relax a little," she continued. "Alright. You're good to go. Take care of yourself and your results on the HIV test were negative."

Standing from his chair, Triple J walked to the door to exit. Both Green team officers were waiting for him outside. One of them grabbed his hand and clamped a red band around his wrist.

"Go over there and have a seat," the jailer told him.

In the section with Central Booking Intake painted on the overhang, Triple J took a seat on the large rubber sofa chair with the other guys waiting.

"They got you pretty good out there, young man," a big bearded older guy said to Triple J. Not trying to talk to anyone, Triple J kept his silence.

"This must be your first time, young man? What you just got was an initiation and now you can tell everybody you've been put down."

"Put down in what?" Triple J looked over at him and asked.

"The club with everybody else down here that's got their asses kicked," he said and laughed.

"Oh, this is one issue you don't have to worry about happening again with me, Old School. Everybody not a lame."

"Ah hahaha," he laughed out loud. "What's your name, young man?"

"Triple J," he answered.

"Excuse me, Triple J. I'm not trying to offend you, but I used to be young and dumb just like you. I've been doing time since I was thirteen and I'm sixty-three now. I used to be a bad man, arms big as a double wide trailer, but do you see me now? These cracker niggers came in with that real hurt team and broke me in half. Be smart, young man. You can't beat these boys. They work for Uncle Sam. He hired them to break you, boy. Stay low in here, do your time, then go home to your family. You hear me?"

"I hear ya, OG, and I hate any of them things ever happened to you, but I ain't been in and out of jail since I was thirteen. I helped my old man count a quarter of a million dollars cash money when I was thirteen. What I'm trying to tell you is everybody down here ain't lame. Ask about me. I'm Triple J, the King of the Apes," he said loud enough for everybody to hear the King was in the building.

Triple J slid over several chairs, running from the funk coming off the homeless guy in front of him. He was one of the real downtown Broad Street crack smoking junkies, smelling just like beer, shit, and hot piss.

"I heard you talking down there Unk. Are you Triple J, Big Homie Ape?" a young voice asked from over his shoulder.

Triple J turned around to get a look at him. He saw the Ape tattoo under his right eye and remembered the young guy's face from somewhere.

"Don't worry about shit, Big Homie Ape. That shit handled. ANW run this bitch," he continued when he saw Triple J's face.

"Run it, huh? What's your name?" Triple J asked.

"Ape Shit Jack!" he said loudly. He was overexcited, damn near screaming, causing many people to look over at them.

"Calm down, Ape. This our conversation," Triple J told

him. Jack leaned over to the side of his head and spoke in a whisper tone.

"My fault, but you know we go Ape shit everyday over here, Big Homie Ape. I promise I didn't know that was you 12 jumped on. Give the word and we'll set this bitch on fire," Ape Shit Jack said, raising up in his chair, ready to go.

"Let me ask you something, Jack. Where were you before you became made?" Triple J asked, quizzing him of his knowledge.

"In the dark. On the shitty side of everything."

"And then?"

"And then things got bright when I was lifted to the moon."

"Now that you're made, how are you supposed to move?"

"Cautiously through the trees."

"On everything, Jack. On everything. You're made and you have to move that way cautiously. Think about the rest of your brothers. If we buss a move in here, we all fucked. We run the streets, Ape. And got a better chance at winning the war on our jungle floor, not theirs," Triple J told him. "How many brothers do you think we have down here?"

"It's some hunters over there," he said, turning towards one of the holding cells." And more upstairs on the floor. Ape Shit Mikko over there with the mop. He's a trustee."

Triple J looked over to the direction where Jack was looking and saw there were about 9 or 10 of his soldiers throwing ANW up on their hands. He saw he had the numbers for a jailhouse makeover, red paint smeared across the wall with pig blood, but nothing good would come out of that for his people.

Many of the ones currently locked up now realized. Triple J's main focus was on his lawyer fees and bond money.

The green suits situation would be taken care of in a matter of time. That was all he needed to know as Triple J continued to sit and talk with Ape Shit Jack as he planned out his next move.

When the light bulb clicked, he realized, Shit Just Got Real.

9

"*D*amn, I been down here three hours and this bitch ain't called nobody name to go up," a young guy in a Mickey Mouse shirt said, losing his patience.

He wasn't the only one complaining, a lot more of them were.

Listening to everyone cry and complain about how long they'd been in intake, Triple J began to worry if he might have to stay a whole lot longer too.

Please, God. Take me away so I can shower and relax, he said in a silent prayer.

Standing from her chair, a tall black woman wearing a burgundy shirt and khaki pants called for him while he was praying.

"Johnson!" she yelled out, looking through the crowd of people. Several guys stood and began walking towards her.

"Which one?" an older guy asked when he realized it was more than one Johnson.

"James Johnson. First name James, last name Johnson," she called out.

"Yes, ma'am," Triple J answered, raising his hand as he stood up.

"Hey, we been out here waiting longer than him," someone in the crowd said.

"And you gone keep waiting, so shut up," she said to him. "Mr. Johnson, please excuse him for being rude. I need you to come up here and have a seat in booth three," she instructed Triple J.

"Yes ma'am," he replied politely as he walked up.

"They got me rushing with you. Say you gotta be upstairs before count, so let's get started." Breaking a record, she literally rushed him through booking, pre-trial interview, fingerprints, photos, and his shower, before making and on his way up the elevator all in 33 minutes.

Stripped of all his clothes, Triple J was dressed in a 3X navy blue jumpsuit with Fulton Jail Inmate on the back andand black and white shower shoes. On his way to the elevators, the female deputy gave him a white net bag with his bed rolled inside. Struggling to hold the bag in his cuffed hands, Triple J wrestled with the bag all the way upstairs.

"Why you smiling so hard? You must be nervous," his female escort asked as they were stepping off the elevator.

"Nervous? Naw, should I be?" Triple J asked.

She looked down at the paper in her hand and then back at him.

"You should be good. You with ANW."

"With ANW? You don't know who I am? I'm King Ape," he said, looking to impress her.

"Yeah, yeah. You know how many niggas try that same shit with me? Everybody say they the boss, but don't even have a business card. Lame ass niggas.

"And anyways, my brother best friend with ANW. He a

boss ass nigga for real with a long check. He already told me Triple J over everybody, but you'll never see him," she said and laughed. "I met everything in here except an astronaut. Y'all lame ass niggas come up here trying to impress me and ain't nothing but JAIL—Just Another Inmate Lying."

Triple J laughed aloud at first for being chomped off after impersonating himself. Learning another lesson in jail, Triple J remembered what his father taught him when he was young. *To catch a sucker, you must first play a sucker.*

Humbling himself, Triple J got quiet.

She'll soon find out that not everybody in jail was just another inmate lying, he said to himself.

"Six North," the tower officer said over the intercom as they approached the burnt orange door.

"Open 900 tower. I'm bringing one from intake," she said, looking Triple J up and down, popping her neck.

The door began sliding on its automatic belt and they walked through. He took him to the right and then they made another right into 700.

When they walked in, the first person they saw was Triple J's nephew, Pooh Man, standing by the stairs with a dust mop handle in his hand.

"My mothafucking, Uncle Triple J. What in the hell you doing up here?" Pooh Man asked him.

"You know they been wanting me, nephew," Triple J replied.

It was a real shocker to run right into his sister's son first on the floor. Pooh Man was gone for a few years now and looked a whole lot different without his dreads. With a beard and bald head, Triple J wondered if being locked up had stressed Pooh Man so much that he had lost all his hair.

"Wait right here, Johnson. I'll be right back," his escort said as she cringed walking away.

She rushed into the office several feet away from them, and Triple J recognized that she ain't moved that fast since they'd been together.

Thinking to himself as he watched her, *Ooh, now she feeling some type of way after all those lame ass niggas. Just another inmate lying shit she'd just kicked. Women, we can't do nothing with them and we damn sure can't do nothing without them.*

"My got damn nephew. How long you been locked up now?" Triple J asked, turning to Pooh Man.

"58 months today. Almost five years."

"And you been in the county the whole time?"

"Hell yeah," he said, shaking his head. "This the drag session, Unk. Everybody down here riding, waiting to go to trial. I had a mistrial and I'm just waiting for the Supreme Court to make a ruling."

"How you have a mistrial?" Triple J asked, curious to know.

"The prosecutor did some illegal shit in court, my lawyer objected to it and the judge declared it a mistrial. It's looking good for me, my lawyer filed a motion, saying that if we have to go to trial a second time, that would constitute as double jeopardy."

"Damn," was all Triple J said, looking over his nephew.

It's amazing how much a person could change within a few years. As Triple J listened to him talk, he remembered the first day his sister brought him home.

"I'm praying with you, nephew. I didn't know what was going on with you. Every time I asked your mama what you needed, she said you was good. You know how Suh is."

"Yeah, I been good. Really having my way down here, eating free world food every day, hustling and getting the pack in here and there. Nun too major, keeping myself afloat," he said. "Now, what the hell you doing in here, Unk? I ain't never known you to get your hands dirty."

"And I still don't. Somebody been burning candles to get me off the streets. It's a lil misunderstanding, I'll be out real soon. You know I'm a federal nigga. Having real paper, we buy out the state."

"True, I know how that go. You see how long I been sitting down here. It's like a hundred some dollars a day they make off us down here. They done made plenty off me since I been down here five years."

"It's a business, nephew. I got stock in Bob Barker, the folks that make all the uniforms, shoes, blankets and toothbrushes. They make damn near everything in this bitch. That's why I was teaching you about investing in the stock market when you was young because if I'm in here or out there I get paid, Pooh."

"They don't call me Pooh down here, Unk. You know I'm Ock now. My name Nasir."

"Oh yeah? That's why you rocking the beard and bald head?" Triple J asked in between his laugh.

"Hahahaha! Hell yeah."

"So, which one you gone sell? Bean pies or magazines when you get out?" Triple J asked him as they both laughed. "I can see you now with the suit and bow tie standing on the corner with a megaphone. The brother minister said 'Hide your kids, hide your wife. Whitie coming to take our lives,'" Triple J continued the joke as they laughed together.

"That's the Nation of Islam, Unk. The same folks that

killed Malcolm X. I'm Sunni. We don't look at them as being Muslim," Nasir said.

Peeking out the office with another female officer behind her, Triple J's escort returned interrupting them.

"Enough with y'all lil family reunion. You know I just looked you up, James Johnson, Junior. You really think you somebody since they got news cameras all over yo' ass Triple J," she said sarcastically.

"You looking niggas up now? Let me find out you choosing to off my Uncle, pimping with all that extra hair flipping shit you doing," Nasir said. "Did you see something you like?" Nasir asked her.

"Gone, Pooh Man. He can talk for his self," she said, rolling her neck, "What you in our video for anyways?" she asked, rolling her eyes.

Triple J found her flattering, laughing at the both of them. He was thinking she looked like his baby niece, Leah just then. Triple J had really made up his mind to let her float on when she dissed him, but now she'd gotten his attention.

She's really not that bad looking, he thought to himself. *She has the mindset of a child rolling her eyes, but I can make something out of her. She's choosing and over thang. I'm just glad she's chosen pimping.*

Triple J looked at her and remembered what his OG potna, King Philly Bo, used to always say to him, "Spare none, Buss your gun". So, since she wanna get caught, a real player might as well catch her.

She stared at him waiting for him to say something. Nasir walked away, pushing his dust mop across the floor, giving them their space.

"In the Bible, there's a scripture that says you never know when you're in the presence of an Angel. Before you looked me up, I was just another inmate lying, but when I saw you, I knew to be polite and say thank you. I've been around the world, seen many pretty girls and despite it all, I landed right here with you. The word destiny and purpose have two different meanings, but in so many ways, they're alike. You may not understand what's going on right now, but you will," Triple J said to her encouragingly.

"What does that mean?"

"You don't understand because you don't want to. Look at me and ask yourself. What's missing?"

"What, you don't have on no socks?" she asked jokingly.

Triple J didn't give her the reaction she was looking for, stoned face the entire time.

"If all you see missing, is my socks, then maybe you should get me some. Some boxers too because I don't have any of them neither. And after that, bring your ass, because I want that too, since that's all you see missing," he replied angrily.

"It's not like that, Triple J," she whined.

"It is like that because when I see you, I see us and nothing else is left. A future with me I can prophetically promise is profitable and if you don't see yourself missing from the dinner table of winners, then maybe you should stay where you at. Do what you been doing, chomping off these suckers. I mean the inmates that's just lying."

She looked at him and continued to cringe. Triple J laid down that real pimp game, not giving her time to think.

"This the real deal, not the rappers and actors. Add it up, not divide and subtract," he continued. "All praise goes to the Ape God and if you can believe in your heart that all Wolves go to heaven, then maybe we can make room for you. Now, I can't save you if you don't wanna be saved and I can't pay you if you don't wanna be paid. Think about that and let me go. I'm sleepy for real."

She paused and thought for a second, staring at him strangely as she deciphered her thoughts.

"When you've worked down here for as long as I have, you hear all types of lies. You're much different from what I'm used to," she said in a soft-spoken tone.

"Indeed, I am."

"Okay, I got you. Come on, I'll take you to your dorm."

Slightly shocked, Triple J saw he had got her thinking. The recipe his OG pimping potna taught him, Triple J always remembered.

"There's never a hum bug or fluke, nephew. Everything's been predestined by the Pimp God. Once a hoe let you in her head, the body gone follow like Sleepy Hollow," he told Triple J. And ever since then it's never failed him.

"You gotta grab a mat," she said, pointing behind him.

Triple J turned and saw the large stack of plastic mattresses under the battleship gray stairs. He sat his net bag down, looking to see which one was the thickest as he approached.

"I got it, Unk," Nasir said as he walked up. Pulling one from the middle of the pile, he got his Uncle a good one.

"What dorm he going to?" Nasir asked her.

"500 cell, 502," she replied.

"500! Hell naw. Who put Unk in there?"

"Classification Lieutenant", she responded.

"Damn, Unk. You ain't gone like it in there. That's the Thunder Dorm," Nasir said. "It's gangland in there. Them niggas on lock down now. I'm gone try to get you moved to the dorm with me when Sarge comes in the morning," he continued.

They walked out of 700 to the 500 doorway. As they walked up, the door began to slide open. Triple J seized the opportunity to get one last word with his new bae before he went in.

"When you see me, what you see missing?"

"Nothing because you got me now," she said.

"All of you?", he asked.

"All of me," she replied with a huge smile covering her face.

"Come see me before you go home. I need some boxers and socks," Triple J told her.

The point of no return came when Triple J crossed over the threshold into the dormitory. No one was out and it was quiet when they walked in. Painted across the floor was a large red box around the door with the words "red zone" inside of it.

"Yooo!" someone sang from behind the door as he walked in.

He must have been some type of scout because as soon as he did that, everybody went off behind the door.

"Yooo!"

"Whoop Whoop!"

"Woe!"

"Salem!"

Cell lights all across the dorm started flicking on and many black faces filled the windows. Locked on Triple J, he could feel their heartache and pain locked in those rooms.

Nasir stopped in the middle of the floor and climbed on the table.

"Listen up, I need to tell all y'all something. This my real blood uncle, Triple J, and he King Ape over ANW. Before we have any issues, I want y'all to know if anybody try Unk, Ape shit and Ock shit gone pop shit. And y'all know 12 don't stop shit," his nephew said and climbed off the table.

"Fuck that nigga!" someone yelled from behind the door.

"Naw, nigga. Fuck wit'em and see," Nasir yelled back, looking at the top range.

While Nasir was talking, Triple J stood behind him with his arms folded across his chest, mugging the cells. Even though his nephew was laying down the law, he wanted everybody to look into his eyes and see he too was on that fuck shit. From the top range, someone called out his name.

"Junior! What's up, nigga? This New Money Cleve," he said.

"Oh, shit! What's up, Ape?" Triple J replied, looking up to see what cell he was in.

New Money Cleve was one of Triple J's personal potnas. They first met when Cleve's Uncle, Lil Hot, had picked him up at the Atlanta Bus station after Cleve had gotten out of prison the first time. On that day, they instantly clicked and ever since then, they'd been like blood brothers.

Knowing Cleve's good hustling ass was in the dorm with him, Triple J knew he could get proactive really quick in here, especially since he'd already caught a lil bae that's ready to go.

Walking to the end of the bottom range, Triple J went to his cell. When he got there and the cell doors opened, he paused because, Shit Just Got Real.

10

*S*tanding at the door stunned at who he'd seen, Triple J stared in shock. Cooler than Cool Joe Brown sitting on the cell sink, Triple J's homeboy from the sandbox, Bugg, stared out at him. The last time they saw each other was when they were in third grade. Bugg's parents had split and he moved to Carver Homes with his grandma.

"What in the hell is my executive homeboy doing in here?" Bugg asked Triple J.

Stunned, shocked, and still surprised, Triple J just stared back at him. So much had changed since they were kids from his face to his voice. But some things never changed. Bugg was always the coolest out of their Grant Park Apes crew. And he was a magician when it came to catching girls. As a matter of fact, Bugg caught one of Triple J's elementary crushes, Starlet Stevenson. After the initial shock wore off, Triple J recovered, landing back on earth.

"You know it don't matter how much money we get, or how well we do in society, we still niggers in a society corrupt by systematic racism," Triple J said.

"Look at you sounding all political and shit," Bugg said, cracking a joke on Triple J.

They both laughed. Even Nasir found humor in the joke about his uncle.

"I see you still got jokes," Triple J replied.

Through some of their mutual homeboys, Triple J had heard Bugg went down the road and did a 10-year bid. Every time they were supposed to link up, something came up, throwing them off course.

"What the hell you doing back in here?" Triple J asked.

"Shawty, I'm good. Just a lil bull shit probation violation. I was supposed to been off this shit two years ago, but the judge keeps resetting me. Me and Missy got to arguing and the old lady downstairs called 12. We ain't even fight and I still got locked up. I'm glad now, because I'm here wit' my motherfucking potna!" Bugg said, dapping Triple J's hand up.

"You know this cool as nigga Bugg, Unk?" Nasir asked.

"Hell yeah. Me and this nigga rode home from the hospital together. Born on the same day."

"Who son this is?" Bugg asked.

"My sister, Mika. This her oldest son, Pooh Man."

"You talking about your light skinned sister with the long pretty hair?" Bugg asked.

"Yeah, this her son", Triple J answered Bugg.

"Aite, Unk, I'm finna' slide. Before I go in for lockdown, I'm gone send you some food."

"Preshate that, nephew. Call your mama and tell her to let Jessica know we up here together."

"Aite, Unk," he replied before he left. The cell door closed behind them and Bugg climbed off the toilet-sink.

"So how much time they gave you?" Triple J asked Bugg.

"Just sixty days," Bugg replied nonchalantly.

"Sixty days!" exclaimed Triple J.

"Yeah! Sixty days ain't shit, shawty. I grew up in Alto" Bugg responded.

"I know, but damn. Sixty days is a lot for arguing," Triple J said.

Thinking to himself, Triple J realized that no matter what you do, once you're in the system, you're convicted of every crime that you're suspected of from then on. No matter if you did it or not.

"Probation a motherfucker," Bugg said.

"How much longer you got?" asked Triple J.

Bugg responded, "Thirteen days and a wake up."

"Oh, I can do that smooth sail," Triple J said.

"Yeah, county time is the worst, though. I wish the judge would have sent me down the road to do it. It's a whole lot better."

"Now what the hell are you doing down here with the wolves? You suppose to keep the name clean."

"Yeah, I know. Man, they charged me with conspiracy and felony murder. Some shit I don't even know nothing about," Triple J said.

Bugg paused and looked at him with a surprise look on his face.

"You got a body?" he asked, voice filled with sadness.

"Yeah," Triple J replied, not really understanding why his voice tone changed.

"Man, Triple J. All these lil niggas up here with bodies," he said. "My bunkie left last night with double Life and twenty-five. Young nigga left not even knowing what all that time meant."

As Bugg talked, reality began to sink in. First time in jail, Triple J was lost and needed to learn the ropes quickly.

"I know you've done time, Bugg, and even though I got a fire ass lawyer, if I have to sit for a minute, what you think I need to know?"

Bugg looked at him and shook his head from side to side.

"Shawty, you my homeboy from the sandbox and out of everybody, I never thought I would see you in here. I ain't gone be here long and you need to know how this shit goes. Fulton jail is the worst county jail in the southeastern part of the United States. It's called baby chain gang because~~its~~ chain gang rules are in effect.

Whatever you thought you seen, you didn't, and whatever you heard, don't repeat it. That means mind your business because if you don't, they gone kill you. Fuck 12 if they ask you anything, shawty. You don't know shit, you ain't seen shit, you ain't heard, just like the streets.

Shit happens really quick in here, so stay on high alert. Niggas down here popping out the cells running in the room robbing and stealing, so ain't no sleep. Don't get comfortable. All you do is temporarily close your eyes. This shit slime down here for real. Niggas act cool, but the whole time, they're trying to peep what you got, find out who you are, and get what they can get.

This the concrete jungle and you got predators and prey, men and gays, stand up guys, and ones that lay. It's really all up to you how you do time. Here, you need this," Bugg said, pulling a six-inch, makeshift knife from his waistband.

Bugg handed it to Triple J and he checked it out. Pricking his finger with the sharp and pointed edge, Triple J squeezed the white cloth handle.

"You gone have to buss a nigga down here," he continued. "When you do, the rest of them gone fall in line. Remember, everybody up here got violent charges, death penalty and life sentence cases. A lot of people up here will never see the streets again, so always remember it's killed or be killed. So, whenever somebody try you, do 'em and do 'em all the way in. You'll be alright here and down the road."

Already fighting a body, Triple J looked at the knife and thought about the fact he might have to kill someone. As the reality kicked in, he realized,

Shit Just Got Real.

11

Triple J's first night in jail was nothing like what he'd imagined it would be. For someone who had never been incarcerated, he would have thought it was just a street nigga's vacation. Time for them to detox, work out and get back to the money. At least that's what Triple J had thought. His first night on the inside and he had already had a wake-up call as a crime boss.

This place is horrible and nothing's about it is cool, he thought to himself as he laid back on the bunk. *"I don't see why people would wanna live like this. I'm locked in a five by nine cinder block, freezing cold jail cell, double bunk, metal desk with no chair and a one-piece toilet and sink. Five steps from the bunk to the cell door is all the walking room a person has.*

Triple J began to think about Jessica, too and it was like Bugg knew.

"Shawty, you talk to your girl yet?" he asked him.

"Naw, I was trying to downstairs, but they rushed me up here. When do we get to use the phones?"

"We can't right now, but I got you."

Bugg reached underneath the bunk and pulled something from behind it. When he got to the cell door, he yelled to someone down range.

"Mookie, send me a bag of chips," he said through the crack of the door.

"Who that is? Bugg?" Mookie asked.

"Yeah, Shawty."

"Oh, aite. The only ones I got already opened, but they still got a lot in there. I'll send you some though. Send me the line," Mookie replied back.

Even though they're on lock down, they were still able to make things happen.

Bugg held what looked like an ink pen with a lot of string rolled around it. Attached to the string was a flatten tube of toothpaste with green writing on it.

Bugg unwound the string, dropping the excess to the floor, and held maybe a foot of the string above the tooth-paste tube. Twisting in circles about ten times, he allowed the tube to pick up speed, Bugg let go and it shot out under the door. Sliding sideways across the floor, everyone could hear it go.

"You see it," Bugg yelled under the door.

"Yea, let me pull it in," Mookie yelled back.

Surprised and amazed, Triple J watched him closely so he could pick up on the skills he was going to need to survive incarceration. While Bugg looked through the crack of the door, the string tightened, pulling the excess string off the floor. Several seconds passed and you could hear the tube sliding back across the floor.

"Aite, you good," Mookie yelled.

Bugg pulled the line in, reeling it like he's on the lake fish-ing, pulling, and winding the string in.

When he saw it was outside the door, Bugg reached down to the bottom of the cell door and shook it several times until the chip bag came in. Inside the bag, he pulled out a white sock. Inside the sock, he pulled out a black and red flip phone. Triple J looked at it surprised. Although it had new age service, the technology was old.

"I ain't seen no flip phone in a long time. Anybody got an iPhone they wanna sell?" Triple J asked.

"iPhone? Naw, but they got some touchscreens in here. I don't think anything for sale right now, shawty," Bugg said as he handed it over. "I'll leave this one with you so you can buss your jugs on but right now, call ya baby."

Checking the time, it was 10:49 and Jess was usually asleep, but he called her anyway. Connecting the call, Jessica answered on the second ring.

"Hello," she said with sadness in her voice like she'd been crying.

"Hello. Hello, baby. Can you hear me?" Triple J said in a whispered tone, not trying to speak loudly.

"Who is this playing on my phone with this baby shit?" Jessica responded, snapping mad.

"Baby, it's me. This me Jess," Triple J said louder, so she could hear him.

"Daddy! Where are you? Are you good?"

"Yeah! I'm fine, just got upstairs. Ready to get out of here."

"I know, Daddy. I talked to TJ. He said they don't have much of a case on you. He promised me that he's gone get you out. Where are you now? Auntie Mary is waiting for you to get a bond so she can come get you. Everybody worried about you, calling your phone since they saw you on the news."

When Jessica started talking, she took off without taking

87

a second to breathe. Certain words she said so fast, Triple J needed a second or two to decipher what they meant.

"I'm at the Fulton jail off Bankhead on the 6th floor. I'm in the Thunder Dorm 500—" Before he could finish, Jess turned into a full ride or die chick.

"Be careful, Daddy," she said. "I know you gone handle your business. Just don't let these suckers trick you, okay?"

"That's right, baby. I'm good."

"I know you are. I been on the jail website looking you up, but they don't have you on there yet. I set up a Secures account and put fifty dollars on there, so you got minutes to call me. I'm getting dressed now. I'm on the way down there to put some money on your books. Make sure you order you some commissary, so you don't have to eat that nasty food. When my cousin was locked up, he made pockets, burritos, and nacho kits. You a boss for real, Daddy, so don't eat that dog food. I'm gone make sure you still live like a King in there, you hear me?"

Jessica was telling him everything about jail like she'd been locked up before.

"Calm down, Mama. I'm fine. I'm more worried about you. How you doing?"

Jessica paused for a few seconds before she spoke.

"I been crying," she said, pausing to take in another deep breath. "But I'm better now hearing from you finally," she continued.

"Don't cry so much, baby. I want you to save some of them tears for when I get out," he said, making her smile.

James and Jessica were husband and wife but also best friends. They did everything together, from community events to throwing upper echelons mansion parties. They were so cool together, Jessica even brought home celebrity models for them to have threesomes with and all. She knew that Triple J loved her, but every chance he got, he made sure to let her know.

"From the very first day that we met, I knew I was in love with you. I just wanna say thank you, Jessie, for being the best wife any man could ever ask for. You've always shown up when I needed you and now that I need you the most, you've shown up and showed out," he said.

"Yeesss, sirrrr!" she sang out jokingly. "You better know it. This is what a wife is for. To love you during the good times and the bad ones. Death shall do us apart through thick and thin, remember that," she said.

"We in this for the long haul," Triple J said, finishing their favorite song. "Listen, our dorm is on lock down and we're stuck in the cells right now. I need to make a couple more calls. I'm gone hit you back before the end of the night. Okay, love?"

"Yes, Daddy," she said sadly

"What's wrong?"

"A lot! I miss you so much already and I just want you to come home. You have a good heart, always blessing those in need and you make sure everybody eats. We're going through this together and I want you to always remember I'm yours and no matter what we ten toes on these hoes."

"That's right. Ten toes on these hoes," Triple J repeated, while laughing at her.

Jessica's one of the realest women he'd ever met. She grew up in a good household and the love he had for her was immeasurable. One thing James Jay taught his son when he was growing up was to be down with who's down with you.

"You'll see who's really with you when the times get hard," Triple J remembered his father telling him.

Now that he was facing a crisis, here was the time to see the difference between the real and the fake. Triple J had to end the call with Jess so he could make some important calls. Now that he had his hands on a phone, he had to see to it that something was done about that incident downstairs.

Looking up into the sky trying to remember the number to his lieutenant, Triple J paused with the phone in his hand for several seconds before it came clear to him. As he waited for an answer, Triple J knew one thing about his hunters' crew. They stayed ready to put in work.

One thing they knew for sure is when Triple J called one in, they would most definitely receive an added job bonus from the boss. Cautious over the phone, Triple J spoke in code so that if Homeland Security or Bugg were listening, all they could say was he was having a party.

"They think it's over for me, Ape," he said to his lieutenant. "Man, I need y'all to throw a big celebration for me, let everybody know that even though King Ape gone, ANW still runs the city. Make sure you get the green balloons for the party and let them go into the air. The big one's like we had last time at the all-white party," Triple J said, chuckling. "We gone call that same white hoe everybody liked and let her MC the party for us," Triple J continued to tell them.

Ending the call after several minutes, Triple J laid down knowing time was ticking for the guys that jumped him in intake. It was time to have a party for them.

Shit Just Got Real.

Coded Conversation Translation:

Triple J referred to the cops as balloons because for some reason their heads blow up real big when they get the job.

Funerals were referred to as home going celebrations, and Triple J referred to murders as parties. The white female MC he'd instructed them to call is a local news reporter that covers a lot of high-profile cases. He mentioned her because he wanted to see it on the news.

12

---

he 23:30 security rounds rattled Triple J when Officer Perry shined the bright ass flashlight in his face. Waking up with a boner, he climbed off the rack and checked the window before taking a piss. No one else was there when he looked out, but as soon as he got to draining the main vein, a knock on the window surprised him, causing him to jerk and get piss all over the toilet seat.

"Bae," a female's voice called out.

When Triple J saw who it was, his face dropped but a huge smile spread across her face as she looked down.

"I like that," she said, referring to Triple J's piss pole after he wiped the toilet and washed his hand.

"I woke up like this. I woke up like this," Triple J replied, singing the lyrics to Beyonce's radio hit single.

"Ummhmm," she said, licking her lips. "I bet you thought I forgot about you, didn't you?" she asked.

Triple J looked back at Bugg and saw he was still asleep.

"Yeah, really I did," he whispered back.

"Well, I didn't. I had to get you some boxers and socks,

bae," she continued, licking her lips at him through the cell door window.

Kneeling down to the floor, she slid him three pairs of white crew neck t-shirts, three boxer briefs and three pairs of socks. As Triple J pulled everything in, he knew that on camera, this didn't look right as she got on her real hot girl shit.

"I'm sorry it took so long. I had to find a store open to get you some. I gotta go. Love you!" she said before she took off from the door.

"A!" he yelled at her and knocked on the window, calling her back, "It's respect! Love leads to tears, respect lasts for years," he told her.

"Respect," she said like a Jamaican, then took off.

Triple J watched her from the crack of the window as she left, thinking she was not Jessica, but she was willing to better the cause.

"Shawty, you don't bullshit," Bugg said. "Everybody been trying to catch Ms. James."

Triple J didn't say anything back because it was Bugg that told him in here, you see and don't see, hear, and don't hear. One thing he was glad to know now was shawty's name, because all he knew her as was the girl who chose pimping. In a major way Triple J was glad she came back with those socks because he needed them in his freezing cold cell.

Quickly sliding into the socks, boxers and t-shirt, Triple J climbed back under the cover, laying back down. As he adjusted to the security rounds, he finally was able to relax his mind just a little. But once again, he was still shaken up when all the cell doors began to open in unison.

Quick on his feet, Bugg jumped off the top bunk and shot straight to the cell door. Covering the doorway, he stood with his hand, clutching his banger as he looked in both directions of the dorm. Triple J moved quickly behind him, making sure to grab his knife off the edge of the bed, as well.

"It's gotta be like 3 in the morning and these folks are serving breakfast trays." Triple J told Bugg. Last night, Bugg had told him they got their trays at the door since they were on lock down.

"I guess we off lock down," Bugg replied, looking around the dorm.

A newbie to lock up, Triple J followed Bugg's lead, putting his back against the wall next to his.

"Single file line when y'all come around," Officer Perry said.

The guys in the cell next to Triple J's led off first and the rest of the line followed. While they were turning the corner at the edge of the dorm coming around, two guys slid around Triple J and Bugg.

Oh, they just jumping the line, trying me to see what I'm gone do, Triple J thought to himself.

Remembering what Bugg told him, *you gotta go in when they try you,* Triple J began to pull the tool out and buss one of them until Bugg grabbed him and pulled him to the wall.

"What the fuck you got going on?" Triple J asked him.

Wham, Wham, Wham, Wham!

When Triple J turned around, he saw the guys that jumped in front of him swinging the long pieces of sharp metal, bussing the one guy that was in front of them and Bugg in the line. He was in shock.

The man getting stabbed tried to run, but they pinned him in, cutting off every escape route he had available. Unable to fight off the knife-bearing men, he balled up on the ground and fell into the fetal position. He covered his head while one continued to stick him as the other kicked him in the back of the head. Triple J pulled his knife out and tried to help the dude since the officers ran off and left, but Bugg pulled him back to the wall with him.

"Stay out of that shit, Triple J. For real, stay out of it," Bugg told him.

Triple J looked up at the top range of cell doors that were still closed. It seemed like everyone was out. A Large majority of the people were behind them punching and kicking the doors, cheering the violence on.

"Eat blood! Eat!" many of them yelled.

On the other side of the dorm, guys stormed the tray cart, snatching trays just to throw them on the floor. More tools started to swing, and blood began to fling all over the floor and walls. One young guy ran up the stairs to the top range, then started jumping up and down on the rails, laughing and screaming hysterically.

Things had gone from 0 to 100 really quick in this Fulton jail. The way Bugg was reacting and responding with Triple J, these were everyday actions. As Triple J continued to look around the dorm, he wished he could call his attorney now because he had to get him the hell out of there ASAP.

Shit Just Got Real.

arching down the hallways, stumping their tactical boots, several riot dressed jailers halted outside of the 500 entrance standing in two single file lines. They shot a gas canister under the door.

Pooof!

The fumes from the glass canister span across the room floor in circles. Bugg grabbed Triple J and snatched him down to the floor with his uniform shirt over his face. The officer in the tower instructed everyone to get down on the floor, while the riot team waited outside the door in formation. Several guys continued to buck, running to the door ready for a fight when the jail staff decided to come in. As the main door began to slide open, everyone was surprised when the gunshots went off from the emergency door direction.

Wabooom, Wabooom, Wabooom! The loud echoes burst through the building's walls from a shotgun dispersing three rounds of rubber bullets.

Several riot officers rushed in from both directions

behind the glass, holding shock shields with "Corrections" written across the front of them.

"Everybody get on the fucking ground," they yelled through their black gas masks.

Triple J and Bugg were already down on the floor, along with several other smart guys. But the ones standing near the entrance weren't so lucky. They were trampled over quickly when the jail staff rushed in beating them with batons and kicking them with their boots. They were even electrocuted by the Corrections shock shield.

A lucky few were able to retreat when the officers came in, the rest were riddled by the pepper balls that were fired by the two-armed jailers who stood on the tables like bank robbers. Overwhelming the dormitory with a large force of staff, Triple J saw maybe twenty or so other officers rush in behind them, but the damage was done.

Laid sprawled across the floor with his head as big as a pumpkin was the guy they'd popped off on first. Both of his eyes were swollen around the head as he looked out into space like he'd already taken his last breath.

The tear gas canisters that were fired had everyone gagging and coughing, even the guys on the top range who still never made it out of their cells. Several jailers moved through quickly after one of the ranking staff members gave the order to bound everyone's hands with zip-ties and to check for stab wounds.

Everyone with injuries was left on the floor while the uninjured were dragged by their arms to the dormitory's entrance. Several medical nurses came in and set up triage, treating the guys whose wounds were worse. One guy was rushed out on a hospital stretcher dead or damn near.

"Hold your breath," Bugg said as one of the combat dressed officers walked towards them.

On that bullshit, he walked through spraying guys on the floor in the face with an orange chemical from a large black handheld container.

Squish!

He sprayed all over the side of Triple J's face, sending a fierce burn through his body, like the tear gas wasn't enough. As Triple J tried to wipe it on his shirt, he was kicked violently in the abdomen by a second jailer that stood behind him. With no choice but to inhale the strong chemical, Triple J gasped for air, instantly coughing out his lungs.

"Didn't I say don't move, bitch,!" the muffed mask-wearing officer screamed. "Y'all gone learn who run this motherfucker," he continued ranting.

Through the coughing, tears and cries, Triple J laid on the floor in pain.

I know anywhere else in the world this would be illegal, chemical warfare, he thought to himself. *But in here, who cares? We're just a bunch of lawless criminals awaiting trial for breaking the law anyways. This is what we get for getting in trouble. Getting our asses kicked, sprayed with dangerous chemicals and unfair treatment is all a part of our punishment. What ever happened to the eighth amendment against cruel and unusual punishment,* he continued to ask himself.

"Get yo' ass up," the jailer that kicked him yelled as he grabbed Triple J's arms.

With his arms already zipped behind his back, the riot officers dragged Triple J across the floor like a chick wing in hot sauce.

Triple J went without resisting even though his eyes were burning like a California wildfire. He was taken out of the dormitory to the small rec yard on the floor in 800. Thinking it would be better to be there, he soon wished he was back in the dormitory where the air had hit him. He was faced with a new burning sensation from the air mixed with the sweat that spread across his face that caused Triple J to scream.

"Aaghhhhh! Fuckkk! Disss shitt burns!"

One of the ladies from the medical staff heard him screaming as he went into the rec yard and saved the day.

"Let me see him," she said. Squirting his face with clear liquid from a circular container like the ones a boxing trainer uses to hydrate his athlete, she cleaned around Triple J's eyes.

"Thank you, thank you, thank you," he said repeatedly, somewhat relieved of the burning pain.

Now that he was able to see, Triple J saw five or six other guys already on the rec yard. Facing the walls with their hands bound and on their knees, he saw them and thought about how uncomfortable they looked.

"All you bitches coming in with all that bitch ass shit, face the damn wall and don't talk. Whoever think they bad, try me I'm gone blast ya ass," the large statured, pepper ball gun bearing guard said standing behind them.

"On ya knees, cross your legs and face the wall," the riot jailer walking Triple J said as he was lowered to the floor. Immediately, he saw what he thought was absolutely true. He was uncomfortable. His hands were bound behind his back overlapping his feet as he knelt on the concrete facing a smoke gray wall. Each time Triple J tried to lower himself on his legs, a sharp pain shot across his chest and he rose back up. The fumes from the spray on his clothes continued to choke him and each time he inhaled the burn in his nose intensified. While Triple J continued to fight to get comfortable, two black guys dressed in black shirts and green pants walk into the rec yard.

"Who sleeps on 502 bottom bunk," one of them asked.

Triple J looked back, and they instantly walked towards him.

"Johnson, that's you?" he asked like he'd known Triple J for years.

"Yes sir," he answered nervously.

Quickly, they rushed over to Triple J and he just knew he was about to get beat up again for some reason. Surprisingly, he didn't. They lifted him to his feet and walked him inside the building.

"You just got here and already fucking up," one of them said as they started walking.

"It's not looking good for you neither. You better pray he don't die Johnson, or you got bigger problems," the second one said.

"Pray who don't die?" he asked, looking to his left as they walked.

On his shirt, Triple J read the yellow letters stitched on the right side that said DART Investigator.

"You know who. That man you stabbed a thousand damn times. He told us you and the bloods been threatening him. He told us you did it on his way to the hospital. Plus, we found a bloody shank in cell 502, bottom bunk. Your cell and under your mat."

Triple J knew it was some bullshit, but his best bet right now was to keep quiet.

Ever since Texas, shit just continued to get realer and realer for him.

"Somebody's got a real hard on for me," he said to himself. "They just wanna see me fucked all the way up."

In pain as he walked to the 700 office for questioning, Triple J continued to cough from the spray. As he walked in, it was no surprise who he saw— Captain James.

"Not Johnson," he said as soon as he saw Triple J. "Come on, man. You have every prominent person in the city trying to get you out right now and you going out bad."

"I had nothing to do with that incident, sir," Triple J replied, truthfully, staring Captain James in the eyes. As he stared back at Triple J, he began to wave his finger at him.

"You know the police detective warned me about you and if it wasn't for the phone calls I've been receiving from almost, if not, every prominent figure in Atlanta, I would have thought you was lying. I was on my way to the floor to move you into a better dormitory, then I get an emergency radio call saying you've damn near killed a man."

"Like I said, I ain't have nothing to do with that," Triple J said.

"Well, tell me who did," Captain James said.

"I ain't no snitch!" Triple J yelled at him. "I'm telling you I ain't have shit to do with any of that. And any more questions you have, direct them to my attorney, Torris J. Esquire." Captain James looked at him and went off into an angry rant.

"This my motherfucking jail and since you so bad, y'all take his ass downstairs and charge him with aggravated assault," Captain James yelled at the DART Investigators, standing next to Triple J.

Damn, Shit Just Got Real.

14

*A*fter being fingerprinted and receiving new charges, shit just continued to get real for the crime boss. As he stared at the back of the elevator after being hauled down to intake getting booked on aggravated assault charges, he began to question if his new charges were because he had a chance to help the man but didn't.

"Welcome to the penthouse," the officer said as they stepped off the elevator to the seventh floor. "I don't know why they had you on the 6th floor, but you should be good now since this is where you belong," he continued.

Fulton jail's seventh floor was one of the most dangerous of all the floors for any county jail in the southeast region of the United States. Most people that went up there never made it off. So many have died on this floor by homicide or either suicide, that most of the jail staff didn't even wanna work on the haunted floor.

Several years ago, a shooting took place at the county's courthouse where a man took one of the deputies' guns and fled on foot. He shot and killed several of the courtrooms staff', multiple deputies and even took out a judge. He became one of the most feared inmates in Fulton jail's history, so much so that the sheriff had a special cell constructed just to hold him inside.

It was nicknamed the metal room because it didn't have any windows and everything inside was welded to the floor and reinforced by six-inch steel. A metal cage was placed around the cell so he could shower and use the phone from his cell.

This cell was never used unless the jail was overcrowded. The only guys that went inside that cell were the most dangerous, violent, and feared. Today's incident has made Triple J that special guy.

He looked around after the jailers uncuffed him and, surprisingly, to Triple J it was much cleaner than his last one. The floors weren't scratched up, both lights worked, and the sink's water worked a whole lot better than the last one.

As Triple J continued to look around, he thought to himself, *I should have been here first. This really not so bad. I need a space by myself so I can work.*

He saw the bunk was different. It had stainless steel and was made for one man. It also was made up like a professional maid service. The blankets were folded neatly, with the corners at the edge of the bed creased and everything was clean. Triple J laid back on the bunk, hoping to get a piece of mind after the series of events that took place this morning.

"I never imagined jail would be like this," he said to himself. "But I'm here now and just as shit got real. I'm gone show who's the realest. Just watch me."

Deep in thought, Triple J heard the guys in the dormitory yelling for him through the cell doors.

"A shawty that just came in. What dorm you just came from?" someone asked, but he ignored him.

"I ain't really trying to make no friends in this shit," he said to himself, "I got enough going on already in my head after this morning. I just wanna enjoy being locked in by myself for right now. All the outside shit is irrelevant."

It was a struggle for him to get comfortable in the new cell. Everything was stainless steel and he was laying on the thin piece of plastic mat. He didn't know if his back was going to survive it if he had to do some time. As he laid there, a knock at the door grabbed his attention.

"A shawty? You didn't hear me ask what dorm you came from," a tall, light skinned guy whose face was difficult to make out asked him.

"Naw," Triple J answered.

"I said what dorm you came from?" he asked a second time.

"Ion know. It was on the sixth floor," Triple J said, shrugging his shoulders.

"Oh, you was down there in that riot. That's cool. You trying to make a pocket homie?" he asked, looking around Triple J's cell.

"Naw, I'm good. I don't sow clothes," he answered nonchalantly.

"What?" the guy asked him. "I ain't talm 'bout no damn clothes. I'm talm 'bout a pocket. Do you got some soups and some chips? We add hot water, let it lock up and make a pocket," he said as he continued to look around the cell.

One thing the crime boss took seriously was eating at the table with unworthy men. He didn't even know the guy's name and he wanted to break bread. Triple J saw he was on that bullshit and tried to send him on his way.

"I'm good on all the small talk, dog. I'm just trying to lay here and chill," he said, laying back down.

"Say what?" he asked aggressively. "Small talk. You must don't think I'll come in der and pour yo' ass out foe gen' smart with me," he continued to say, tapping against the cell door window with a makeshift metal knife.

Immediately, he got Triple J's attention when he began to wiggle the cell door and pop the automatic lock. Manually sliding the door quickly, he rushed inside, catching Triple J totally off guard. Unable to get up fast enough, Triple J struggled to lift his arms as he prepared to block the downward knife swing aimed straight at his face.

Working extra hard not to get stuck, he tried everything to move, but for some reason, he couldn't. Twisting at the hips quickly, he turned to the side so he could get a kickoff, but his but his legs wouldn't move.

Caught totally down bad, he saw the armed man coming down with the arrowhead pointed knife at his face. As the knife lowered, he continued to fight the paralysis state, trying not to get stuck, but his body still wouldn't move. Accepting his defeat, Triple J closed his eyes and thought right before the knife banged him in the face, Damn, Shit Just Got Real.

nock, Knock, Knock.

"Mr. Johnson, sir. I need you to get up and get dressed for your first court appearance, sir," a female's voice said, waking Triple J up.

Jumping to his feet quickly, Triple J scanned the cell with his hands raised, ready to hook. Beads of sweat ran down his forehead, neck, and chest. As he took deep breaths, his chest heaved heavily up and down. When Triple J realized there was no one in there but him, he exhaled heavily, thankful it was all just a dream.

Still in defense mode, he disregarded the black and white shower shoes issued to him and walked to the cell door barefooted. From the corner of the wall, Triple J looked out the window to see whose shadows were waving under the door. Immediately, he saw a beautiful, female sheriff's deputy. She was 5'5" in stature with pretty hazel brown eyes, no more than 135 pounds, with beautiful pecan brown skin that glowed like the heavens up above.

"Oh my God, she's beautiful," Triple J said as he turned closer to the door.

On her shirt, Triple J looked down at the gold nameplate tag that rested on her breast and smiled.

"Lieutenant Rodgers," he says to himself. "The only woman who has ever made me sweat like this I married," he continued.

Lt. Rodgers saw the attraction he had for her and blushed, showing the light purple braces on her pretty, white teeth.

"Mr. Johnson, I need you to hurry and get dressed so we can get you to your first appearance in court," she said. "And, please, put on your shirt," she continued, staring down at his chiseled abdomen.

Lt. Rodgers bit down on her bottom lip slightly as Triple J turned away. The connection between the both of them was electrifying and they both felt it. Triple J tried to control himself and say no, but his body continued to say yes.

Jeeerrrrtttt.

His mans transformed into full action mode, stretching out the front of his pants with an erection. As he threw on his shirt, Triple J prayed it was long enough to cover his embarrassment because Lt. Rodgers had three male deputies with her outside and this wouldn't look good in front of them.

Right as Triple J stepped to the door, one of them stepped up to the door. Standing next to Lt. Rodgers with black handcuffs in his hand, he instructed Triple J to turn around and cuff up through the open tray flap. Seeing the look on his face Lt. Rodgers stepped up and took over, cuffing him to the front. One hand at a time, she placed the cuffs lightly around his wrist, then closed the tray flap.

"Seven South Tower, open cell 618," she said into her walkie talkie mic attached to her shoulder.

With this new extreme hatred for male cops, Triple J stood at the door with his game face on as it slid open.

"Good morning, Mr. Johnson. I'm Lieutenant Rodgers and we're here to escort you to court safely today," she said, singing in her soft melodic voice, "Captain James told us your rough stuff and you need to be cuffed behind the back, but I ain't doing all that. You gone be on your best behavior for me, right?" she asked seductively, blinking her eyes rapidly as she stared at him. Triple J's mouth turned to a smile quickly.

"Yes, ma'am. I don't know why the Captain would tell you something like that. I been on chill," Triple J replied and chuckled.

"Okay, I trust you," she said, leaning over towards Triple J. "We gone talk later about that stabbing this morning and find out if you really been on chill," she said sarcastically.

"Yes, ma'am. But I was charged with it and I'm going to tell you like I told the Captain. I don't wanna discuss any legal matters without my attorney present."

"Your lawyer is downstairs," she said as she brought him out of the metal cage.

Before they descended down the stairs, Lt. Rodgers slid her arm into his like they were going on a date. Quickly, she realized what she'd done and pulled her arm out, gripping around his triceps.

"Watch your step, Mr. Johnson, these stairs can be slippery sometimes. Especially wearing those cheap shower shoes, "I don't want us to fall," she said, blushing and pausing a few seconds. "In love," she whispered in his ear when they reached the bottom of the stairs.

This woman is crazy, Triple J thought to himself. *But she's my kind of crazy.*

One of the male officers held on to his left arm as they walked down the stairs. Lt. Rodgers instructed the officer to go ahead in front of them once they reached the bottom. Together, Triple J and Lt. Rodgers walked out into the hall together. She walked him near the 900 exit door then spoke into the intercom.

"Tower, I have inmate Johnson from cell 618 going to his first court appearance. I need you to sign him out and send down his three cards," she said.

Several seconds passed by and Triple J couldn't seem to take his eyes off her.

Staring at her assets, he eye fucked her the entire time they stood there. A white plastic container attached to a multicolored rope, fell down a tubing system connected to the tower behind them. Lt. Rodgers reached in and grabbed a piece of paper from it before they exited.

Through the 900 doorway, down the hall to the elevators, they walked to meet up with the other deputies. As they approached, the three deputies were laughing while in conversation. One of them typed in a series of numbers on a silver keypad outside of the elevator and each time he pressed a key, it beeped. Loud noise came from the elevator's shaft as it began to come and several seconds later the doors behind them slid open.

Before Triple J stepped on, Lt. Rodgers continued to flirt. She slid his hands from in front of his wood and brushed her plump cotton soft ass across his lap, pressing back.

Triple J looked up in the sky as she looked back at him smiling.

"Step to the back of the elevator," one of the male officers said, pointing with his finger. "And face the wall."

He stood behind Triple J while the others hung on to the handrails around the elevator walls. The doors opened and they stepped off onto the second floor making a right, then a quick left around the corner. Triple J was taken to the end of the hallway and stopped in front of the attorney booths.

"Your attorney is here, Mr. Johnson. He wants to see you before we go inside," Lt Rodger said.

One of the male officers pulled out a set of keys from his pocket, unlocked the door and Triple J stepped inside. The attorney booth was separated by cinder block walls and three-inch reinforced glass. Triple J sat alone on the metal stool as he waited for TJ to come in. As TJ entered, his mind began to wonder if he had any good news yet, because after last night, he was most definitely ready to get home.

Racing thoughts filled Triple J's mind, he looked up as TJ was bending the corner. Dressed to impress like always, TJ wore a navy blue, pinstriped suit with a gold multicolored stripe tie. If he ever decided to change his profession, TJ could easily become a magazine model. TJ sat across from Triple J, on the freedom side of the glass window.

"Mr. Johnson, what's going on? What are these new charges about?" he asked.

"TJ, man," he said, then took a deep breath. "This is the worst place I've ever been in life. You gotta get me out of here like yesterday," he said with an urgency in his voice, "Last night, they put me in the worst dormitory in the jail. They call it the thunder dorm. While we were going to get breakfast trays, some guys lost it and the stabbing went digital. I had nothing to do with it, but they trying to say the dude identified me on his way to the hospital. I lawyered up on the Captain when he asked me about it and he got upset and told the investigators to charge me," Triple J told his attorney.

While he was talking, TJ was taking notes, writing on his yellow legal pad.

"Which Captain?" TJ asked with his pin on the pad.

"James," he said.

"Alright, we're not going in for that case today, but I'm going to make some calls and see to it that it goes away, Mr. Johnson. In the meantime, I need you to be cool and stay under the radar. We have enough already on our hands and anything extra is detrimental not beneficial. The prosecution team is trying to build a case on you and anything they can use to make you look bad in front of a jury, they will. We're not going to give them what they want, so I need you to help me Mr. Johnson, and stay out of trouble so we can get you out."

"I'm with you, T.J.," Triple J replied.

"Alright. Let's go in here and do this," T.J. said.

―――――――――

"This next case is James Johnson Junior versus The State," the prosecutor read aloud.

"Mr. Johnson, you're being charged with conspiracy to commit murder. I'm not allowed to give you a bond today, but you'll have the opportunity two weeks from now in superior court," the female black judge said to him.

The court deputy gave T.J. a pink piece of paper who then handed it to Triple J, the judge had written on it in black ink, "BOND DENIED!"

A box checked at the bottom of the page had advised him

that his case had been bound over to Superior Court on the side of it. Seated in the visitation booth, Triple J saw his Jessie Pooh. She sat behind him dressed beautifully in a two-piece, navy blue Louis V pants business suit with the matching handbag. When the news cameras weren't on Triple J, they were on her. Jessica maintained her facial reactions when Triple J's bond was denied. She loved her husband but refused to allow the media to see her sweat.

Lt. Rodgers snatched his arm, dragging him out of the back of the courtroom, through a packed holding tank.

"Who is that woman that was sitting in the back there for you?" she asked, rolling her eyes.

Triple J looked at her and knew, Shit Just Got Real.

16

"I asked you a question, James. Who is that woman?" she asked him for a second time.

Triple J looked at her in shock because this is the first time Lt. Rodgers called him by his first name as he thought, *How is she gone question my pimping?*

Lt. Rodgers continued to stare at him, placing her hand on her hip.

"My wife," he answered, laughing at her sinister facial expressions.

"She's gorgeous," Lt. Rodgers said, rolling her eyes as she let out a strong sigh.

Triple J nodded his head up and down agreeing, Jessica is gorgeous. Lt. Rodgers' reaction was no shock to him. It was actually common.

Straight woman had come up to them in the past and asked to join them in sexual relations. While Lt. Rodgers grilled him in the hallway, the three other officers exited through a second courtroom door further down the hall. When Lt. Rodgers saw them, she turned them away.

"Y'all stay down here and help them with the court escorts," she told them. "I'll take him back upstairs," she continued.

"Are you sure, ma'am?" one of them asked.

"Yes! I'm good. Johnson don't want no problem with me. Do you?" she asked, bucking her shoulders at him.

"No ma'am. No problem at all," he replied, chuckling at her.

"That's right. I ain't got my 5.11s on today, but I'll still kick his ass in these patent leathers," she said, blushing with twinkle-twinkle little stars in her eyes as she stared at him.

Lt. Rodgers grabbed him by the arm and took off up the hallway with Triple J.

As they were walking, they took a different route. Instead of taking him directly upstairs, she took him down a long hallway. At the end, they went through a set of battleship gray doors.

Lt. Rodgers placed him against the wall as she typed a code into the silver keypad to get through the magnetically locked doors. She then dragged him inside to the administrative offices. For the first time since being locked up, Triple J saw sunlight and colorful walls.

Ahead of them, standing at a copy machine, was a beautiful young woman with thick track star legs bulging through her dark brown skirt. Triple J made eye contact with her as they passed. She locked eyes with him and smiled.

"Good morning, Megan," Lt. Rodgers said as they were walking by. "I gotta conduct a quick interview in my office with Inmate Johnson about the incident that happened this morning."

"Yes, ma'am. I got you," Megan said, shaking her head up and down.

They entered Lt. Rodgers office and Triple J looked around quickly.

"Have a seat," she told him, pointing at the pinewood stained cushioned chair.

She took a seat on the opposite side of her desk. "Now, tell me what happened this morning in dorm 500 and don't lie."

Without giving him a chance to speak, she took off.

"I don't wanna hear that shit," she yelled, confusing him as she stood up, slamming her hands on the desk.

Damn, he thought to himself. All day things have been going good and now she's gone Level 3 Mental Health.

Lt. Rodgers walked around her desk and headed towards the door. As she came around, Triple J's heart began to beat rapidly through his shirt.

"Now you better tell me everything and don't leave nothing out," she continued to yell as she closed the door to her office. Triple J sat in his chair, then turned with his eyebrows raised as she began to unbuckle her belt. She dropped her pants around her ankles, then bent over and took off her shoes quickly with her assets facing Triple J. Stepping out of her pants, she left them on the floor and walked towards him.

"Mr. Johnson," she said, pausing at the side of his chair. "I don't give a fuck about that bitch if he lives or die. I'm here for you. I want you to know you can do whatever you wanna do to me. Just make sure I get mines first." Triple J looked at her without a response.

Shit Just Got Real.

riple J stared at Lt. Rogers and thought about the last time he was in a position like this. It was back on the plane when the flight attendant pulled up on him. He slick was raped.

As Triple J stared at Lt. Rodgers he thought, *I didn't know when I got locked up that I was going to become a sex slave. This is almost too good to be true, but this shit is real.* Triple J began to think about the things he had in motion. *This just might be the opportunity I need to get it going.*

His attorney just told him to chill and stay under the radar, but for some reason, he couldn't. Lt. Rodgers pulled him up from the chair by the arms and stood him up. Still in handcuffs, she pulled the elastic band on his navy-blue jail bottoms with her left hand and stuck her right hand down the front of his pants.

She removed his limped pole from his pants and pushed him against the desk. Bending at the knees poking her plump ass out towards the door she worked his dick in her hand.

"Damn, this shit feels good," he told her.

She continued to work him in her hand, trying to get him hard. Impatient, she said "Fuck it", before she took the monster cock in her mouth. Kissing the tip of his iceberg, she continued to work it, lapping her tongue in circles around the head.

"Damn. Bitch, you rude," he said, placing his cuffed hands on the top of her braided hair.

Lt. Rodgers looked up at him and smiled as she continued to let him make love to her face. She worked her head back and forth and placed her forehead against his abs.

"Yo' dick growing in my mouf," she said, talking with a mouth full.

Triple J looked down at her and back up, thanking the Pimp God for the oral skills she was gifted with. Her warm and wet lips wrapped around his pole had Triple J thinking she was born to be a dick sucking pro and not 12.

She was going in, sucking and slurping, taking as much as she could, but the struggle was real. Bobbling with her tongue out, she went down gagging, trying to extend her throat and take more in. As soon as Triple J's leg jerked, she immediately stopped and pulled her head back.

"You hard headed," she said, standing up and looking him in the eyes while she continued to work his mans in her hand.

"Don't put the blame on me. You're the one trying to suck the soul out of me" Triple J responded.

"Yeah, yeah," she said, wiping the side of her mouth like she just knew she was fye. Chuckling, "what did I say? I better get mines before you get yours," she continued.

Pulling him away from the desk, she turned him around and propped her right leg up on top of the edge of the desk.

Spreading her big ass cheeks on full moon, she began talking shit.

"Fuck all this talking. Give me some of that thug dick," she said, smacking her ass cheek with her right hand.

Triple J laughed out loud and thought, *Who said I had some thug dick? This woman is crazy, this shit goes Ape Shit.*

Walking up on her, he sang out, "Guudd lawd." Then rubbed circles around her big booty cheeks.

Wasting no time, he slid in her guts, diving in and was immediately weakened at the knees. Lt. Rodgers was a sex vet who knew how to work her pussy muscles. Gripping every inch of his pole with her tight pussy, she got Triple J pussy drunk, slurring at his speech.

"Ohh, oh, ohh, shit," he said out loud, thinking he had to shake that shit off quickly.

Gearing up, Triple J beat across his chest and said, "Play time's over with."

Driving straight in, he long dicked Lt. Rodgers as he gave her that Willie D.

"Oh my God," she screamed and laid her head flat on the desk, knocking some of its contents to the floor.

Triple J continued to pound and was shaken up a little when someone knocked at the door. Pausing in place, he looked back, but the Lieutenant continued to throw her ass back, riding on the pole.

"Is everything okay in there? Sounds like I heard something fall," a female's voice outside the door asked.

"Everything is good. Real good. I apologize for the noise, but I got it all under control," she said while she continued to bounce her ass up and down. "Thank you for checking, hun, but it's all good in here," she said as she looked back at Triple J and smiled, still riding his dick slowly.

Stone solid in the pussy, Triple J made her eyes wander into the back of her head as he continued to give her long back shots.

Clap, clap, clap, clap.

The noises for sure could be heard in the hallway. Triple J tried to hold it down, but she kept throwing her ass back as he threw the dick forward.

"Ohh, ohh, ohh, ohh. Plee—ease don't stop fuu—cking me —e," she said in between back stabs. "Oh my gosh. Don't move. Sta—ay rite der," she continued.

"Is everything good in there?" the female asked a second time, knocking at the door.

"Ya—as, yass, yass. Bitch, dis di—ick is mo—tha fuk—in gud," she screamed.

Triple J laughed and wondered what would happen if the wrong person caught them. Lt. Rodgers continued to throw her ass back and he continued to give her that Willie D. The office door began to open, while he was knee deep in the pussy.

"LT!" the woman from the copy machine screamed as she watched her boss get her guts busted open.

Triple J pulled out and turned towards the secretary with dick hanging.

"Mr. Johnson. Please, put that thang up. You're in here hurting this woman," she said with a smirk on her face.

"Megan, this nigga dick good, girl. You better get you some before he goes back." Lt. Rodgers said, bouncing her booty cheeks up and down. Triple J couldn't think of anything else to do but smile.

They done turned me into a sex slave/boy toy overnight, he thought to himself.

Megan closed the door and started walking towards him, licking her lips.

"Can I have some too?" Megan asked Lt. Rodger in a polite voice.

Triple J smiled at them both as they began to kiss.

"Y'all some nasty lil sluts," Triple J said as he pulled up Megan's brown skirt.

Snatching off her black lace panties, he stared at the side by side fat and pretty, police bitches with their asses tooted up in front of him on the desk. Looking up at the sky as he pressed his hands together, Triple J said, "All praise to the Pimp God. You shole do fuck with my pimping."

As soon as he got two good backstabs in Megan's good pussy, the door swung open. Staring at him with his hand on his gun holster, was the devil himself—Captain James.

Damn, Shit Just Got Real.

18

"Okay, Mr. Johnson! I see you think you can just come in my facility and do what you wanna do," Captain James said, shaking his head. "First, you stick my inmates. Now you sticking my sta—ff," he said in between, taking a breath.

Triple J broke down quicker than grease lightning on the toughest stain, while he was still talking.

"Ple—ease find your pants and put that thang up," Captain James continued, shaking his head from left to right after checking Triple J's limp dick out.

Lt. Rodgers climbed off the desk and grabbed his jail bottoms, helping him to slide them on. While she was pulling them up his leg, she licked his stomach with her freaky ass and mumbled under her breath, "Thank you."

Captain James grabbed Triple J by the arm and pulled him out of the office as Ms. Megan trailed behind them with a multi-emotional look on her face and an embarrassing blush.

As they were leaving, out Lt. Rodgers yelled at Captain

James, "Take his good dick slanging ass back to his cell and don't ever let him out. I'm 'bout to lose my job and house trying to bond his slick ass out."

Captain James continued to drag him out as Triple J prepared himself for the worst. Every time he and the Captain had an encounter, it never was for something good.

Shit always got real.

They walked down several doors to Captain James's office before he threw Triple J down in a chair identical to the one Lt. Rodgers had in her office.

"So, Mr. Johnson. I see you're enjoying your stay here at the Fulton Jail," Captain James said, seated across from him at his desk.

He took off his glasses and sat them on his desk. Staring at Triple J, he tried to look through him, but Triple J stared back just as hard as he did. The last time they talked, Triple J didn't say much, exercising his right to remain silent, and this time he promised himself to do the same.

Anything I say to this guy will be used against me in the court of law, so my best bet is to remain silent, he thought to himself.

"Listen, Mr. Johnson," Captain James began to say. "I know we got off to a bad start, but I'm going to fix it. I told Ms. Rodgers to take you to court today and make sure you were happy before we take you back to your cell."

Triple J continued to look through him with zero change in his facial expression.

"Okay, tough guy," he said.

Captain James picked up his desk phone and dialed a number. When it started to ring, he turned it towards Triple J.

"Torris J. Esquire," the called person answered. Triple J recognized his attorney's voice as soon as he answered.

"Torris. What's up, man? This is Marvin," Captain James said.

"Marvin! What's up, man? I just left from down there. I was going to call you after shift."

"Yeah, I heard you were here. I was trying to catch you when I got caught up on the line with the DA's office. I didn't know Triple J was your mans. He's here in my office with me now."

"Yeah," T.J. said.

"Yeah, I gotta tell you he's hard as a rock."

"Diamond in the rough," T.J. replied, referring to his client.

"This morning, Johnson got mistaken for another guy that damn near killed one of my other inmates. Those new charges were dropped, and I wanted to personally let you know in front of him that he has nothing else to worry about with that situation."

"Thank you, Marvin. Mr. Johnson is one of my best clients and I appreciate you for taking care of him. I'll be by the lighthouse to see you soon."

"Light work. Do you need to speak to him, Mr. Johnson?" Captain James asked Triple J.

"Naw, I'm good," Triple J answered, still staring through Captain James.

Captain James ended the call and turned the phone back towards himself. He leaned back in his chair, clasping his hands on the center of his overgrown watermelon belly and stared at Triple J.

"Your father-in-law called this morning and asked me to get you whatever you needed while you were in here. You know we have a lot of mutual friends in this city that hold high seats. And these times can be highly lucrative for the both of us if you're willing to work for me," Captain James said.

While Captain James was talking Triple J thought to himself, *I don't work for nobody, but there is a way we can collaborate.*

His old man, James Jay, always told him, "It's better to collaborate then compete."

"I'm offering you the greatest deal of your life," Captain James continued. "And if you give me your word, I'll make sure you see some of the best days anybody has ever seen incarcerated."

Triple J listened, but it was all just a bunch of gibberish, in one ear and out the other.

"Hear me out, Mr. Johnson," Captain James continued, raising in his chair and leaning forward. "I put in a move slip for you to move across the hall in dorm 100. Last night, a tip came into our central office from an outside source that has our entire administrative staff on edge. As you saw this morning, shit gets real down here.

In dorm 100, things are heating up and a war between your ANW guys and the Bloods will pop off when they come off lock down if someone with real influence like yourself doesn't intervene. If this war happens, it's going to spread around the jail like a wildfire and I'm sure it will reach the streets.

Johnson, I really need you to help prevent me from having to haul another how many ambulances away like we did this morning. I know you can put a stop to this and in return for your cooperation, I'll give you a treat and a bonus."

"Hahaha," he laughed out loud, unable to hold back the loud outburst. "You give treats to dogs when they roll over

SHIT JUST GOT REAL

and sit. Is that what you take me for, Captain James?" Triple J asked as he continued to stare through him.

"I'm sorry, but I'm not that man and I damn sure didn't get locked up to become a jailhouse ambassador. To be honest, I think it's best we let the lil' homies work things out the way they do," Triple J said, declining the sucker and lollipop that Captain James offered to him.

Triple J knew his response was not the one Captain James expected, but what was he expecting? If he thought the crime boss was about to become a slave laborer, sorting out problems for the police, he had to be retarded. A jailhouse war would be right up his alley right now, especially with all the stress he's feeling.

One thing Triple J knew was that his Apes and Wolves were gone handle business if it came down to it. Going Ape shit is right up their alley.

Captain James stood from his seat and walked around his desk, sitting in the chair next to Triple J.

"Mr. Johnson, I respect the fact that you live by the G-Code and I'm with you on that. I ain't gone snitch on my homies, as y'all call them, if it comes down to it. But this is bigger than you and me. It's bigger than them and us. This is about humanity. Young Black Lives.

We have so many young black men killing one another each day because the OGs in the game sit back and turn their heads like we don't see what's going on. Now I know you think I'm the enemy because I wear this uniform and shield. And I know the system is corrupt, but when I wake up I'm just like you, a black man.

When I see young black men gunned down in the streets that affects me just like the Black Lives Matter movement. I see young black men dying every day. The ones killed and the killers I have to send down that road to the DOC for life.

The only way for us to save our black race is for good men like us to show them a different way of life. You wanna know why I do this? It's to save the generations to come by showing them something different," Captain James said, staring deep into Triple J's eyes.

They stared deep at each other, looking deep into one another's soul. Captain James' eyes showed compassion deep down in his heart as if he really did care. Everything he said to Triple J was true, but a lot of the young guys weren't ready for that change. They didn't give a fuck about shit, especially the one's in Fulton jail because they knew they were going to be gone for the rest of their lives.

The peace talk Captain James prayed for, madeTriple J wonder how he was going to do it. This pain ran way deeper than what Captain James and his administrative buddies saw. What they saw didn't even scratch the surface. When Captain James extended his hands to shake his, Triple J just stared at him with no emotion on his face.

He's asking for my help to save these young black brothers' lives. I don't know how but I'm gone do it, Triple J thought to himself as he reached out and took the Captain's hand.

Shit Just Got Real.

19

7 South, Dorm 100

riple J walked in and the first thing that came to his mind was, *Damn, Captain James really set me up this time.*

Triple J felt the intense energy in the room and it didn't sit right with him.

It was liable to really pop off at the drop of a dime and he felt it.

"You're going to cell 108," the officer said as he walked in.

The cell began to open and standing in the doorway was another one of his personal Apes, Ape Shit Flamez, standing with a knife to his side. On the street, Triple J knew Flamez to be on some playa shit with the women, but Ape didn't play any games when it came to the family. When Flamez saw Triple J, his face lit up and he rushed out of the cell.

"Triple J," he lightly screamed, meeting the crime boss in the middle of the day room. "Let me get this," Flamez said while grabbing the plastic mat and throwing it on his shoulder.

Quickly, Flamez toted the mat into his cell, throwing it on the open bottom bunk.

Triple J immediately realized there was something not good about the bottom bunk since neither Bugg nor Flamez wanted to sleep on it.

"Triple J! What's up? This Ape Shit Jack," his lil homie yelled from down range.

"What's up, Ape? I'm gone get up with you when we come out," Triple J replied, looking down his way.

The dorm got loud, and everybody started calling his name.

"A, Triple J? Triple J?" several guys called out.

"Say, Flamez? That's King Ape down there with you?" another person asked as the cell door closed.

"Yeah, Ape!" he said as he went and got up with everybody when they came out.

"Aite, Ape."

Triple J smiled, but in a way, he felt bad. He was oblivious to the fact that he had so many little homies behind the barbed wire fence. It was enough of them in Fulton jail to create an entire new chapter of ANW.

"You know you was all over the news yesterday and last night, Ape?" Flamez said to Triple J.

"Cameras was all over me, Ape!" Triple J said.

"Really, though. I wanna know what in the hell is The Executive Homeboy doing in here with the wolves?" Flamez asked him, waving his hand around the room.

"You know I'm an international nigga, Ape. I'm everywhere like natural air," Triple J replied jokingly.

Flamez gave Triple J the same surprised stare Triple J

gave him when he came in. It wasn't an everyday thing one of them got to share a cell with the King Ape.

"It's good to see you but not like this. We at war right now. You need this," Flamez said, passing Triple J a second knife from his waistband. "We coming out bussing second rotation, and you gone need this, Ape."

Triple J took the sharpened metal from him, gripping tight around with its cloth woven handle. Examining it closely, Triple J twisted it from left to right, checking it out.

To the naked eye, it looked good enough to stand through the fire. The arrowhead point was sharp on each side and sturdy.

"If need be, this gone open a bitch up," Triple J said to Flamez.

"Yeah, flame a bitch up," Flamez replied, smiling.

Triple J started having flashbacks about the situation downstairs. *I'll be damned if I let a motherfucker sixth floor me*, he thought to himself. Flamez had a long piece of strings hanging from the knife's handle. Triple J grabbed it naturally, wrapping it three times around his wrist, tucking the excess string under the wrap.

"You know what you doing with that?" Flamez asked.

"You just better know what you doing," Triple J replied, staring at him.

Flamez steadied his eyes out the cell window, looking around the dorm like he was seeing some type of movement.

"What the hell you got going on, that you gotta be looking out the window?" Triple J asked.

"I told you when the doors pop, we pop!"

"I'm with that. Now tell me what we popping about?"

"The homie Wiz Wolf gave one the Bloods up here one, about two weeks ago and slime don't wanna accept his loss.

He sent a SOS, Smash On Sight, out on all of ANW, declaring war on us. One of the Apes intercepted the scribe and sent word up here to us. So, when the doors pop, we pop," Flamez said.

"Come on, man. Really? All this about a fistfight? We have too much paperwork to be beefing bout some bull shit like this, Flamez. What type of business are we running down here?"

"Ween got shit going on up here."

"And why is that? We got ANW on every floor and ain't nobody got nothing going on up here."

"They do. It just ain't enough for all of us to eat like on the streets."

"Come on, Flamez. We supply two-thirds of the city and ain't nobody called to get right? My first day in this bitch I got a bitch to go buy me polo boxers and draws and hand deliver them to me."

"These niggas not rocking right in here," Flamez said.

"Da fuck you mean not rocking right? It's only one way to rock and that's to the ANW beat," Triple J said, standing in front of the bunk staring at Flamez. "You've known me for a long time. You were there during the merger, you saw how we put two killer crews together. Now you telling me you can't manage a jailhouse?" Triple J asked, upset.

Triple J was upset because they managed to stretch ANW to other states and they're doing way better than his own A-Town crew. Time is money and Triple J couldn't grasp in his mind the idea that they were about to go to war over some lil boy shit.

"I rather be back in the cell by myself than to listen to this," he told Flamez. Even though he was upset with Flamez, he realized most of the blame went to him.

It's no way in the world my apes are ever supposed to be down here fucked up, he thought as he sat back down on the bed. *We in the A where everything started. How does this make me look? I'm Triple J, King of the Apes, and my Apes and Wolves down here broke and 'bout to set off a whole war about a fist fight.*

Even though he told Captain James he was no jailhouse ambassador, he really appreciated him sending him in there. Somebody with some sense had to get this shit under control.

Shit Just Got Real.

20

---

*A*t 3PM sharp, all of the doors began to slide open.
"Count time, count time, count time, gentleman.
Grab everything you need. Your cells will close behind you,"
one of the officers yelled as they walked in. Several guys in
the green suits crew walked in with the floor officers. Immediately, Triple J saw them and thought they were there just in
case things got loco.

Flamez was upset and had that Ape Shit look all over his
face. Pants legs rolled up, towel around his neck, and socks
off, wearing his black and white shower shoes. Flamez was
ready.

A short, black female jailer wearing a gray shirt and black
pants, started at the far end of the dormitory, flipping
through the count book each time she passed a cell. Nobody
said anything as she passed, but the guys on the far end
watched her back-side twist as she moved up the bottom
range. She stopped in front of Triple J and Flamez's cell.

"You're new. Are you Triple J?" she asked, standing like a

model as she posed for a photo, one leg in front of the other, blinking her eyes. The entire bottom range stuck their heads out and looked towards them.

"I'm just Inmate Johnson, ma'am," Triple J replied nonchalantly, making no eye contact with her.

"Okay, that's cool. Be like that then, Inmate Johnson," she said with an attitude, twisting her burger booty away as she walked off.

After checking the last cell on the bottom range, she flipped back the shower curtain, checking it before walking along the wall and up the stairs. One of the guys with the Green Team stared directly at Triple J and walked towards him.

While he approached, Flamez asked, "Da fuck he want?"

It didn't take long for them to find out because he went directly to Triple J.

"Wasn't you involved with that boy getting stabbed downstairs this morning?" he asked.

"No, sir," Triple J replied.

"Don't sir this fuck nigga," Flamez snapped.

Triple J knew Flamez was ready to buss his gun, so he lightly touched his hand to calm him. Triple J had it already in motion for the two of them. They were just waiting for the right time.

"I thought we put him in the metal room, Sarge?" he looked back at his other team members and asked one of them.

The youngest one of the crew answered, "Yeah, that's him. Captain James said to let him out."

He got close to Triple J and half of the bottom range stepped out and headed towards them.

"Back on your cell doors," the other officers yelled, while one stared Triple J in the face.

"We better not have any more problems out of you, or I'm gone make this a rough stay."

"You ain't gone do shit," Flamez said, walking up on him.

The lady officer finished her upstairs rounds at the same time the green team member acted like he wanted to pop. They had back up in the jail, but if they thought now was the time to act up, they had to be fools. Everybody in there had knives and was ready for war.

"Today, your lucky day," he said to Flamez, but little did he know it was actually his. As the officers left and headed to the next dormitory, the cell doors began to close behind them.

"Say, y'all won't this smoke. Let's get it on then," one of the ANW homies yelled as he was coming down the stairs. It was about seven or eight guys trailing closely behind him.

"Ape Shit! Y'all come here," Flamez said, calling everyone in front of their cell behind the stairs. On the other side of the dormitory, the bloods migrated together, gathering in a group. Everyone stood ready with sinister looks on their faces.

Triple J leaned over and asked Flamez who was their leader. Flamez nodded towards the tall light skin guy.

"They call him Big Boo. He's supposedly the OG Blood from New York, but my people up top never heard of him. They say he's locked up for triple homicide, but we don't give no fucks" Flamez said with aggression. "We all in here for the same shit."

"Aite, cool. Y'all stay back. Let me go holla at 'em."

Triple J stepped out in front of his guys staring at Big Boo and his Bloods.

Big Boo stepped up and for several seconds, they just stared at one another. Triple J motioned for the OG's to meet alone in the middle of the day room. It was time for a sit down.

From the look of his eyes, Triple J could tell he was a little hesitant, but that didn't matter. He came in peaceful but was ready for the ape shit. Triple J walked towards the table, extending his hand for them to have a seat. OG Big Boo disregarded the invitation and walked to the middle of the dormitory, stopping under the elevated television.

Triple J saw the preference to stand as disrespect but disregarded it. He was now on the turf and came, specifically, to make peace. Following OG Big Boo's lead, he met him under the television, keeping a six-foot distance.

Both stared at each other, getting a feel for one another. Triple J, being the boss that he was, took the lead in the conversation.

"OG Big Boo, I've heard nothing but good things about you, so I wanted us to talk as men before things got set on fire for some kid shit. I don't know if you know of me or not, but I'm Triple J the King Ape A.K.A. Mr. Make a way. A long time ago, I learned it's a whole lot easier to collaborate than compete. And truly I believe we could save ourselves a whole lot of unnecessary energy if we invested our time with money instead of knives," Triple J said, pausing for a second. "I'm all about the come up, bettering the black race. If you can give me a couple of days, I can promise you our time will be a whole lot easier in here and profitable."

OG Big Boo looked at Triple J and nodded his head up and down.

"I'm not impressed with your little Martin Luther King I have a dream speech you're giving me," OG Big Boo said.

"But it's definitely got my attention 5. Yo, you know the news blasted on you yesterday like you were King Kong or something around this bitch. If you were anyone else, word to motha, I would have bombed on you for bullshitting me and wasting my time. JAIL. J-ust A-nother I-nmate L-ying. Now, the question is, what do you have for me to keep the peace?" he asked Triple J.

"What do I have for you to keep the peace?" Triple J repeated after him and laughed. "I like that. The first thing you're keeping is your life."

OG Big Boo charged Triple J and swung his fist roundabout for the crime boss's head. Efficient in martial arts, Triple J dropped low, pivoting left, and grabbing a hold on the charging bull's arm as he passed. Locking around OG Big Boo's wrist and elbow, Triple J twisted at the hip, swinging his leg out. His foot clipped the raging giant and slammed him to the floor. As he was falling, he looked up at Triple J with his eyeballs popping out the socket.

The Bloods charged to help him but Triple J's crew met them before they could buss a move. Triple J saw them coming and quickly snatched out his knife, pressing it against OG Big Boo's neck.

"I don't know if you know much about the stock market, but jails and prisons are lucrative business," Triple J yelled at Big Boo as he continued their peace talk. "It's plenty of money to be made and if we used our organizations and network together, we could flood this shit with everything from phones to weed and cigarettes," Triple J continued with his knife pressed against Big Boo's neck.

Both crews stood at a standoff and OG Big Boo knew he was in serious trouble if he didn't see things Triple J's way.

"You got a highway?" Big Boo asked, swallowing with the knife pressed against his neck.

"'I'm Triple J, Mr. Make A Way," he said to answer his question. "Downstairs, the going rate for phones were $600 for flips and $1000 for touchscreens. I'll supply the upfront funding, then wholesale a few to you at half of the going rates. This would leave you and your homies plenty of room to eat so that we are all straight. To show you I'm serious about a wealthy future for us, the first ten phones are on me. You'll need six to communicate with your homies on the other floors. One to keep for yourself and do whatever with the other three," Triple J said, encouraging OG Big Boo.

OG Big Boo continued to lay flat on his back, he was calculating the numbers in his head as Triple J pressed the knife more into his neck.

"It sounds like a deal to me," OG Big Boo said, reaching his hand up towards Triple J to seal the deal.

"One more thing," Triple J said.

"What's that?"

"Your lil homie sent out a Smash on Site scribes," Triple J said, looking up at the Bloods, standing in front of him. "That's gotta be dealt with," Triple J told him.

"Done," OG Big Boo said.

Triple J removed the knife from his neck and grabbed OG Bg Boo around his wrist, helping him to his feet.

"I don't know how y'all was moving before I got here but fuck that bullshit. It's over with. We gone get some money in here," Triple J said to the dorm.

He and his guys back peddled back in front of this cell. On the other side of the dormitory, OG Big Boo took his slime that sent out the SOS under the stairs and for five minutes, five guys jumped him in violation.

Triple J and his crew watched as the lil dog took his whooping. OG Big Boo nodded his head at Triple J and Triple J nodded back.

Now that their beef had been killed, it was time to get some money.

Shit Just Got Real.

21

*I*t had been almost 48 hours since Triple J last saw Captain James. The issue with OG Big Boo was killed, and the Captain should be pulling up on him soon. Triple J pressed the gas on the drop after he'd gotten a hold of a burner phone. His only need was to see the Captain.

"Cell 108. Johnson, get dressed, you have an attorney visit," the booth officer called over the intercom. Triple J had just talked to his attorney on the burner and knew he wasn't there to see him.

As he got dressed, gathering himself, he held a surprised look on his face until the cell door slid open. Out into the hall, he walked and waited for him at the 900 door where the man he needed to see was there—Captain James. Captain James cuffed Triple J's hands to the front and took him down the elevators. When he felt it was safe to talk, the Captain broke his silence.

"Mr. Johnson, I wanna thank you for your cooperation on behalf of the jail and all of its staff. If the war between ANW and the Bloods happened, it would have been devastating for everyone, everywhere," Captain James said as they walked down the hall towards his office.

"I didn't do it for you or the jail staff. I did it because they were about to kill each other for some bullshit. OG Big Boo was willing to cease the troubles through a business proposition I offered him which includes you."

"Well let's hear it," the Captain replied.

"This morning, I had a friend misplace a bag he thinks he mistakenly tossed in the trash can while he was down here adding funds to my books. Can you check to see if it's there? I'll appreciate that." Triple J said, looking over at the Captain.

"That's what I wanted to talk to you about, Mr. Johnson. One of the orderlies found that bag this morning and it was not placed in the lost and found. There were some items inside that were not allowed to pass the guard line. I've already processed the property destruction paperwork and evidence sheet," Capt. James said even toned.

"Well, now we have a problem, sir. Your peace treaty you sent me on for humanity was broken with the exchange of ten phones..."

"Ten!" he exclaimed, quickly cutting Triple J off.

"Yes, ten," said Triple J.

"How many did you say your friend lost?" asked the Captain.

"I didn't, but I believe it's in a ballpark number, like thirty-five" responded Triple J.

"Oh my," Captain said, smiling. "Only one of them was destroyed, but I have the bag in my office," Captain James said as he opened his office door.

He stood back so Triple J could walk in first. It was like the stars aligned, and fireworks burst in the air, while air force jets flew over their location.

Usher's hit song, "There Goes My Baby" played in real time as soon as his wife Jessica stood from the Captain's office chair. They rushed to hug each other, planting warm wet kisses in the middle of the room.

"Phat Mama, I miss you," Triple J said before looking over at the Captain.

"I told you if you did that for me, I had a treat that belonged to you. And that trash bag," he pointed to the side of his desk, " that comes from me."

They both smiled at each other, knowing what was inside. Captain James closed his officer door, leaving the two of them alone.

"Jess," he said, surprised to be holding his wife in his arms. "I miss you so much already, bae."

"You must don't miss me enough. You still talking," she said, blushing through her teeth. Jessica fell straight back onto the love seat against the wall of the Captain's office. Triple J fell between her legs, planting more kisses on her thick, pretty brown lips.

"Mmm, daddy. Mmm," she said in between kisses.

Triple J unfastened her pants at the same time, while pulling his mans out. Slowly separating her heavenly gates, he entered her warm hole, feeding her his oversized beef stick.

"Ahhh," Jessica sang out pleasantly, while scratching the back of his neck.

"You miss daddy dick?" he asked her as she took him in her tight little pussy.

"Yas!" she sang as he slowly pumped inside of her. "Yass, daddy. Yass," she continued.

It had been almost a week since they last made love before Triple J's arrest when he banged out her juice pouch.

Even though he'd been fucking off it still seemed like it'd been forever.

Digging deep inside his majesty, driving dick inside her guts, Triple J knocked on her back walls.

"Yes, yes. Ohh, yass. Daddy, you on my spot," she sang out loud, loving the long strokes.

Jess's eyes rolled to the back of her head and her legs shook violently as he continued to plunge.

"Ohhh shiiitt," she screamed, erupting her warm larva heavily.

Triple J continued to plunge, shaking his leg as the warm juices flowed down his leg. Now that she'd gotten hers, it was time for him to get his. Slamming his fist on his chest, Triple J transformed into Willie D. Jessica knew the routine, propping her big ass up on the sofa and sticking her head into the seat cushion with a perfect ass arch.

"It's time to go surfing," Triple J said, laying across her back as he moved his arm like he was on a surfboard.

Diving inside her dick head first, Triple J stood up in the pussy while vaginal juices flowed like ocean waves crashing ashore. As he continued to dig in, his eyes rolled back, and his toes curled into a tight ball. His legs locked up and a blast went off.

Boom!

A busload of unborn babies was dropped off inside her nursery and Jessica looked back at him smiling as she took them in. Pussy drunk, Triple J continued to slow stroke until his dick went limp. Beads of sweat flowed from both Triple J's and Jessica's face.

Jess rolled around, reaching down to grab her designer handbag, and pulled out a pack of baby wipes. Cleaning her husband first, she rubbed softly across him, making sure to kiss the mic before pulling his pants up.

"So, how does it feel to fuck the Mayor's daughter, inmate?" she asked, joking with Triple J as she cleaned herself up.

"I'm sorry, I never knew you were the Mayor's daughter," he replied. "I fell in-love with the girl wearing the cupcake hat," he continued.

"So you say," Jessica replied with a huge smile on her face. She picked up the trash bag off the side of Captain James's desk. "Let me see what we have here," she continued as she untied it.

If it was anybody else getting in his business, Triple J would have blown up. But Jessica was his wife and she was as real as they came. She reached her hands in and pulled out a pound of weed and four cans of cigarettes compressed inside vacuum-sealed bags. Triple J saw the work and thought about his guys upstairs.

Shit Just Got Real.

22

One pound of high-grade marijuana, four cans of tobacco and 34 cell phones were individually wrapped in clear flex-seal. Jessica pulled everything out the bag and went into Trap Queen mode, ripping open the large plastic trash bag and laying it flat across the floor.

"You would have needed some help getting this back, but don't worry, Daddy. I got you," she said as she was operating on the floor. Jessica placed the phones down first and folded them inside the bag along with the weed and cigarettes, tying everything down.

"How you learn to do all this?" he asked her, amazed at her packing and wrapping skills.

"My daddy taught me how to pack a rucksack like he did in the marines," she told Triple J.

Thankful for her, Triple J looked up to the heavens before leaning over planting kisses all over her. Together, they stood up and Jessica reached around him, tying the plastic pack around his abdomen like a waist trainer.

"Got damn. I can't breathe," he said, wrapping his arms around Jessica. He squeezed her when she finished.

"Me neither," she said, whispering to him.

Triple J loosened his grip and smiled before he tongued her down.

Right as they began to get deep into their kiss, a knock at the door interrupted them.

"Knock, knock," the captain said as he knocked on the door. " Mr. Johnson, do you and your attorney need more time?" he asked.

"Uh. No sir," he replied, looking over at Jess. "We were just wrapping things up," he continued speaking literally.

"Alright, Johnson. We gotta leave now," Captain James said, looking at his watch.

The goodbyes and see you laters had always been difficult for the pair, especially now. Jessica's eyes began to rain down tears as they kissed before Triple J had to go away. Captain James gave them as much time as he could together. Even breaking the rules, letting Triple J ride down the elevator with them to the jail's lobby. The last walk away from the elevator, Triple J watched Jessica's backside twist and turn, and it was sexy because he knew she would be back.

Now it was hard watching the elevator doors close in front of them. Silent as they went up the elevator, Captain James placed his arm around Triple J's shoulders.

"I know it hurts and I just wanna say, I appreciate you again. I know we got off to a bad start, but you see how I fixed it. I let you spend some time with your wife and get you right. To be honest, I wish I could look out for every man down here, but every man not like you."

"And what do you mean by that?" Triple J asked.

"They can't keep their mouth closed. You're a powerful

man with strong political connections and you're a part of Atlanta's first family."

"Captain, please don't stroke my ego. I just had to leave my wife to fend for herself. I'm just a little black boy in these cracker eyes," Triple J told him. "But listen, Captain. Back to business. I have an issue."

"What's that?"

"I need to be able to move product to the other floors."

"That's no issue. I've already worked that out for you. We have a sanitation/maintenance detail here and I made sure one of your ANW guys got on the crew this morning. His crew has access to the fifth, sixth, and seventh floors. I been here twenty-six years and I can tell you that's where all the money is," he told Triple J.

Off the elevator, Captain James walked Triple J back to his dormitory, making sure he got to his cell without interference. Triple J walked in and put up the shit flap, covering the cell windows like he was using the toilet. Flamez turned his head to the wall, thinking he was really about to go. When Triple J took off his shirt, he told Flamez to jump down and help him untie the bag, restricting his breathing. Flamez eyes lit up when he saw the drop had come in and they were on like popcorn. Cell phones, cigarettes, and weed laid across the bottom bunk and right then they knew, Shit Just Got Real.

23

Once a hustler, always a hustler and that was something you couldn't ever lose like riding a bike, James Jay, Triple J's old man once told him. He gave him the game raw when he was young and caught his father in the kitchen whipping crack.

"Son, one day when you get older, you're gonna take over the family business. And you gone need to know how these things go," he told him as he invited him to the stove with him.

James Jay even showed his young grasshopper how to count up on the triple beam and work the digital scale too. He gave Triple J lessons on how to cut, weigh, and package the dope, even quizzing him at times to make sure he was listening. He knew his son and he knew he had a liking for nice cars. Instead of confusing him with all the drug talk, he explained the game to the young Triple J in parables so he could grasp everything the Trap God wanted for him and more.

"The small bags were Buick money and the big bags were

Bentleys," Triple J remembered his father telling him.

He wasn't the smartest kid in the world but knew if he wanted anything in life to last, his best bet was to start small and work his way to the top. That was so that he could get a clear understanding and respect for the game.

He reached for the keys, jumping into the drug game, but instead of grabbing the ones to the Bentley he grabbed the ones to the Buick.

Just jumping in the whip, he knew it would be better to take a Buick down the crash course than an expensive Bentley. And today, he appreciated his choice because now he was at the top and the ride was a whole lot smoother.

"Look at us now," Triple J said to Flamez, remembering where they started.

Triple J had the bottom bunk covered with product and it all had to go. First he pulled six 4G Verizon flips out and sat them on the top bunk. Then another 4 4G touch screens.

"These are for OG Big Boo and his crew," Triple J said, keeping his word to their peace agreement. "All a man has is his word and his dick. If his word ain't shit, he ain't shit," Triple J continued telling Flamez.

He had no problem purchasing the phones for them because he knew how important the communication tools were to get things going. Everything was already coming through ANW, so the money he invested on their few Buicks was small change to the Bentley's fare he and his crew would be running up.

Triple J had Flamez buss open the vacuum seal with the tobacco in it. Immediately, the whole cell stunk like a tobacco field on a hot sunny day. They had to hurry up and get things sacked up before the jailers did their security rounds.

"We ain't bombing up nothing but packs," Triple J told Flamez.

A pack of five 30cc medicine cups sold for $100. They sacked the weed up in ounces and when everything was added up, they were looking at a return in profit somewhere in the ballpark of $20,000.

When Triple J saw the numbers, he was satisfied with their first drop. It wasn't much for the crime boss, but enough to make sure his young apes had food to eat and not that beef they were eating when he came in.

Triple J had his attorney working to get him out and knew sometime soon, he may be leaving. Leaving his young apes in a position to keep things going on before he left was the goal and he was sure to make it happen. All evening, they got right activating four of the phones for themselves and the lil apes in the dormitory.

With a few small things left out and everything else put up, Flamez and Triple J got ready for second rotation. The dormitory door started sliding early and Flamez ran to the window to see who was coming in.

"Cuz, where you at?" a voice Triple J was familiar with called out. It was his cousin, Kola Ape. They weren't real cousins, but they always told everyone they were since James Jay and his mama used to call each other brothers and sisters in the drug game.

"Where you at, cuz?" he asked again.

"108, Ape," Triple J answered as he sat up off the bunk. Kola had pull with the tower officer, getting him to open up Triple J's cell. Flames was at the door holding security while Triple J slid into his navy-blue Bob Barker karate kid shoes.

"He good?" Flamez asked Triple J as Kola tried to slide in.

"Yeah, he's family," Triple J told him

"This the great, Kola Ape. You heard me," Kola said as he walked past Flamez.

It was good to see this was who Captain James sent up because Kola was all about the money. As he dapped Triple J up, he slid him a sandwich bag filled with crushed clear looking crystal powder.

"What's this?" Triple J asked.

"Cream."

"Cream?" inquired Triple J.

"Yeah, that's what they call Meth in here," Flamez said.

"Naw, I'm good on this, Ape," he said, handing it back to him. "I got something for you, though."

Triple J didn't want no Meth. Everybody he knew that did that cream shit would stay up for several days and flip out when they were on it. It was already enough going on up on the seventh floor and they didn't need anything extra to bring out the wiggers.

Weed and cigarettes was his thang, everything a person needed to stay calm. .

"You right, cuz. I know you don't need nothing. They told me to come see you. Say you got something for me," Kola said.

"Business as usual. Three packs of CIs, an ounce of green and five phones. Three touches and two flips."

"Hell yea, Ape! What you want back?"

"I want you to be able to re-up. Take care of the young apes down there with you. Bring me $2700 for the lines. You keep one and we good," Triple J told him.

"Hell yeah, I got you," Kola said.

"I'm good. I told you to take care of everybody down there with you," he told Kola when he gave him his package. "One more thing. I need you to take some to my nephew,

Nasir, on the sixth floor and my mans, Bugg, when y'all go down there."

"Yo' mans?" Kola said and paused, looking at Triple J funny. "Bugg from Carver Homes?"

"Yea."

"I heard he booking niggas."

"What you mean?"

"I'm saying everybody that goes in a room with that nigga get booked on a jailhouse testimony. All that hearsay shit be enough to convince the jury of guilt," Kola said and paused again, looking at Triple J. "I hope you didn't tell him nothing about your case?"

"Fuck no! He ain't my lawyer. I don't even know much about this shit as it is. They just got me locked up." Triple J paused, looking into Kola's eyes. "I appreciate the 411, but I still need you to shoot this to him," Triple J said, handing over Bugg's ounce of weed.

Kola looked at him crazy again and shook his head before leaving the cell.

Triple J thought about what Kola had just told him when he laid down.

If Bugg was a rat, why didn't someone get at him when the riot popped off downstairs? It was plenty of opportunity for them to shake something before the police came in, Triple J thought. Niggas will create a lie on a good nigga in a minute just to see him fucked up.

True or false, Bugg was his partner. Triple J knew if Bugg didn't have his back downstairs, he too could have been laid out on the floor or in the hospital bleeding out.

Right or wrong, his loyalty ran deeper than the surface and now was the time to prove it.

Shit Just Got Real.

or the majority of the time, Triple J stayed in his cell handling his outside business while Ape Shit Flamez and the rest of his ANW crew handled the inside business.

Over the phone, he and Jessica communicated constantly as she filled in as his business ambassador. Jessica continued to do a wonderful job keeping the family's business afloat while he was on his involuntary vacation.

Most of Triple J's corporate associates were more excited working with her than him being who her father was, and Triple J knew that. Jessica was no slouch. Since a child, her father had schooled her in the arts of negotiations. A few deals Triple J struggled to close, Jessica sealed them with more than he originally planned.

"The Pimp God has done it again," she said to herself.

Triple J laughed at her trying to talk like he did. While he was laid back on the bunk, he began to reminisce on the day they had met. At the time, Jessica attended the historically black all girls school, Spelman College. After class, she would help out full time at her Aunt Keisha's Cupcake Shop in the Greenbriar Mall food court.

From time to time, Triple J would see her working as he walked through and would think, Damn, she's a real cutie pie.

One evening while passing through, he thought maybe she was off when he didn't see her at her regular spot.

"Guess who?" a female's voice asked after creeping up behind him, covering his eyes with her soft and smooth hands.

"I have no idea," Triple J answered honestly.

"That's why you have to guess," she replied.

"Well, I know it's a female with a beautiful voice and soft hands. I don't recognize the voice, but if I had to guess, it would be Cupcake Hat," he answered.

Jessica chuckled hard and let him go. When Triple J turned around and saw her huge smile staring at him with her twinkle eyes, his heart immediately began to beat fast.

"You're good. How did you know it was me?" she asked.

"Your energy," he said, pausing for a few seconds. "It's different," he continued.

"I wanted to surprise you today. I see you here a lot, but you never have shopping bags. And you're always by yourself."

"What you talking 'bout, woman?" Triple J asked, staring at her with a funny look. "Are you spying on me?"

"No!" she said quickly, slapping Triple J across the shoulder as she continued to chuckle. "Ain't nobody stalking you. I just assumed you worked here because I always see you walking past my Aunt Keisha's cupcake shop. You're always smiling at me, but don't ever speak. Are you shy or something?" Jessica asked him.

"Shy?" Triple J repeated and chuckled. "Naw, I laughed because you're the only one I know that can pull that off."

"Pull what off?" asked Jessica.

"That hat," Triple J said, looking up at her pink and white brimmed cupcake hat.

"Oh, you like that?" she asked, placing her hand on her hip looking at him with an attitude. "Or the girl in the hat?"

"Both," he said, forcing a big and beautiful smile to reappear on her face.

Triple J saw the pretty dimples in her cheeks and liked her even more.

"I'm sorry for being shy," Triple J said, extending his hand out for a handshake. "I'm James Johnson, Junior, but everyone calls me Triple J."

"Nice to meet you, James Johnson, Junior. But everybody calls me Triple J, face ass," she said, jokingly. Jessica knocked his hand out the way, bypassing it to get her a hug.

"My name is Jessica Reeves and I'm not a dude, so don't be trying to give me no handshake," she said firmly, looking up at Triple J still in his arms. "But you can call me Cupcake," she continued, chuckling again as she stepped back.

Triple J stared at her and knew then she was the one for him. Their energy was electromagnetic, drawing them closer together by the second. Jessica stood close to him in line like she also knew they belonged together. Triple J, being the gentleman that he was, asked her to lunch.

"I don't know how long of a break you have, but I'm ordering wings and would love your company. My treat," he said, causing her to blush more, spreading her smile wider.

"You got me fucked up, dude. You can't buy me with no wings. I have my own money," she said, shooting him a curve. Quickly losing her smile, Jessica mean-mugged him like he was really doing something wrong. Triple J stared at her.

This girl must be loonie, he thought to himself.

Most of the females he'd met in the past, expected him to pay for everything, especially on the first date. Jessica was different. Triple J stared at her as they moved up in line silently, thinking to himself, *I like her independence. She's young and beautiful, but there was no way I could let her pay for her own food.*

Slippery as a pimp named Slick Back, he slid back, allowing her to order in front of him.

"Would that be all for you today?" the cashier asked when Jessica was done.

"Yes," she replied and began to reach into her wallet. Triple J moved forward, wrapping his arms around her as he laid his hands flat on the counter.

"Yes, ma'am. And I would like a 15-piece hot with lemon pepper sprinkles."

"I'm sorry, sir. Are you two on the same ticket?" the cashier asked, looking at him strangely.

"Yes, ma'am. Same ticket," Triple J replied.

"I told you I was buying my own food." Jessica replied like she was upset but had a smile on her face when she looked back at him.

"Yes, you did, but neither of us are Dutch, so why should we date in a way so far from the American way?" he asked her in his late night, over the phone voice, lowering himself into her neck.

Jessica couldn't resist the charm, melting in her skin. She could no longer protest and eventually allowed him to pay for their meals together.

"Y'all look so good together," the female cashier said before taking his order.

The lunch date was great; both of them agreed. For dessert, Triple J agreed to have one of her aunt's cupcakes for the first time and Jessica recommended her favorite, the red velvet cupcake, which was a Ciroc-infused cupcake. Triple J ordered two and decided to pay.

"Have a nice day, Mr. Triple J," she said after boxing them up.

"Please, let me pay for them," Triple J insisted, but Jessica refused to take his money.

"You paid for the food, I'm paying for dessert," Jessica said.

"Okay, cool," Triple J said before dropping a twenty-dollar bill in the tip jar and walking off.

"Hey wait!" she yelled. Triple J turned around to see her staring with the saddest but the most beautiful, brown puppy dog eyes.

"You didn't ask for my number," she said. "Please, don't leave without having my number. I won't be able to sleep tonight if I don't hear more from you," she continued, catching him totally off guard.

Triple J was amazed he knew he wanted her but didn't know how to say it. She came straight out with it, no cut, no chaser. Jessica wanted him to know she was calling dibs.

"I don't think I would have been able to sleep tonight without talking to you as well. Please may I have your number and we can continue enjoying each other's conversation later tonight," he asked her nervously like she was going to say no.

"Yes! Now give me your phone," she demanded. "And you got a IPhone. Yes! We can Facetime," she said excitingly.

"Don't nobody wanna see you. I said talk, not video chat."

"Oh really," Jessica replied as she saved her number.

"I'm just playing with you. Don't get all cupcake on me," Triple J said.

"Don't play unless you playing for keeps," she said as she handed him his phone back to him.

"I like you too much already," Triple J told her.

"And that's a good thing," Jessica said as Triple J walked off.

Checking his phone, Triple J saw she saved her contact with all emoji's. It was a lady wearing a wedding dress and two cupcakes on each side of her.

"My cupcake wife," he said, looking back at her, smiling.

———

"Hey, Big head," Triple J said when he saw a text the next morning on his phone.

Jessica had texted him at 5:22AM early before she headed out to class.

Throughout the day, they texted each other and Jessica ended up inviting him to dinner. Jessica told Triple J so much about her father that he felt like he already knew the guy.

Shopping at Fifth's Plaza, he purchased a brand-new Armani suit, Triple J was prepared for the evening. His father always told him that first impressions were the best impressions, so he made sure to put on his best, letting her father know his soon to be son in law was worthy of his daughter.

When Jessica texted the address, Triple J pulled their home up on Google maps. It was a beautiful home on top of a hill, recently purchased by Reeves Investment Group. Triple J knew he had to show up in style, contacting a limo service and ordering a driver to chauffeur him to the house. In a black on black 2010 Cadillac Escalade, customized with black executive leather seats, Triple J rode to her house. When he pulled up to the address, Triple J saw a cop car parked at the edge of the driveway and didn't know what to think.

Her father must be some big mafia dude or something, he thought, looking at the huge house. *Don't tell me I'm fucking with the plug's daughter.*

History would be repeating itself all over if he was. When his father met his mama, he didn't know she was the Cocaine God's daughter. The cop stepped out of his car and stopped them.

"I have Sir James Johnson, Junior here for Ms. Jessica Reeves," his driver said to the cop who waved them along. Granted access up the circular driveway, they drove to the top, breaking at the paved pathway that led to the front door.

"Sir Johnson, enjoy your date," his driver said after opening his door.

Nervous the entire walk to their front door, Triple J didn't know what to think. A sense of relief came to him when Jessica met him at the front door. She was dressed in a beautiful black evening gown with a big red bow on the shoulder.

"You look handsome," she said, smiling. "And you smell incredible," she continued, hugging him tightly.

His father always taught him that when someone visited a man's house, they should wait at the door until they were invited in. Even though Jessica told him it was fine for him to come in, he still stood at the front door until the man of the house showed up.

Walking down the spiral stairs dressed in a black tux with

a white shirt was someone he never expected to ever see there.

It was Atlanta's Mayor Kasim Ramone Reeves.

Triple J looked at Jessica and thought, *I know you're not the Mayor of Atlanta's daughter?*

Shit Just Got Real.

25

*T*hings were going good for Triple J and the product was moving faster than he had expected. Soon, he would need to see the Captain and get his next package since what he had was almost gone.

While Triple J worked his calculations in the cell, he took out the time to educate his young one Flamez.

"I'm gone show you this because in the corporate world, these are things you need to know if an investor asks."

Using a sheet of legal pad paper, Triple J designed two charts. One for profit margin and the other for markups. Flamez needed to know these things since Triple J planned on departing soon. He would need to show the potential profits of their investments.

Flamez watched in amazement as Triple J took him through the steps. Even though this was new information for Flamez, he understood the algebraic equations. His excitement came from being able to sit down with his million-dollar executive homeboy and receive the corporate business education he had to offer.

Triple J saw his hunger and deep down in his heart, he felt Flamez was confident enough to keep things going when he took off.

Looking back, he knew Flamez was a natural born hustler and moved weight up in Baltimore. Even though Triple J hated to offer credit without some collateral, Flamez had a way of managing it right.

"Back home—" Flamez began to say. "—in Baltimore, we sling heroin and when a fiend ask you for credit, you give to them. If you don't and they know you got it, they'll kill you. Simple as that," he told Triple J.

While he was talking, Triple J recalled plenty of corner hustlers that had been killed that same way by dope fiends. One of his high school classmates, Young Richie, was all about his money. That "no credit" policy cost him his life bucking on the wrong junkie.

While they were sitting there talking, Triple J was called out for an attorney's visit in 700.

"Mr. Johnson, how you doing today?" his attorney, Torris J. Esquire, asked him. "I wanted to get down here and update you on everything that's going on. I have to be honest with you. This fire is growing and I'm working overtime to get it contained."

"Okay," Triple J answered him, while nodding his head up and down.

"I have some good news and bad news. I just received a copy of your discovery," T.J. said, holding up a three-inch black binder. "The deputy's going to bring you your copy so you can see what's stacked against us." Triple J continued to nod his head up and down as T.J. briefed him.

"Now the bad news. We won't be in preliminary tomorrow."

"Say what?" Triple J asked quickly.

"I know, I know," T.J. said, trying to calm him. "Last week, the DA's office conducted a secret indictment hearing and the grand jury voted against you," T.J. said. "We both know this case is high profile and truly I expected an indictment to come down. You know your co-defendants have been down here for over ten months. One of them has mentioned your name several times over the jail calls and that's what brought you up in the case—"

"Hold up," he interrupted him. "It's a lot of people that scream Triple J. How can one person get me indicted by mentioning my name in a jail call? And anyways, who is this co-defendant?" Triple J asked.

T.J. looked at him and paused before he responded.

"His name is Joseph Johnson."

"My cousin?" Triple J asked with an astonished expression on his face.

"Yes," T.J. answered him, shaking his head.

Instantly, anger ran through the veins of Triple J. He had gotten so pissed, he banged his fist against the stainless-steel table inside of the attorney booth, shaking up his attorney.

Joseph's supposed to be locked up for aggravated assault, he thought. *How was he able to get me jacked up on murder charges? I gotta get out for sure now before I kill this clown cousin of mine.*

"Aite, T.J. Now give me the good news. How much will the bond be? Will I need cash or property?"

"Mr. Johnson, I planned to ask the judge for one at preliminary. Because you were indicted, I had to file a bond's motion. The good news is I talked to the court clerk and she's added our motion to next month's court calendar. If anything was to come up in the meantime, I give you my word that you'll have one within the next ninety days."

"Ninety damn days!" Triple J yelled. "Come on, T.J. You said two weeks and now this bullshit. I gotta get back to my wife," Triple J continued, standing up and snapping at him.

"I know, Mr. Johnson. I'm upset just as much as you are. Something you have to remember is, this is a murder case we're fighting and things are a whole lot different. You have one of the worst cases you can ever get, and it's already indicted. This doesn't mean you're guilty, but it slows down the process for us," T.J. continued, trying to calm his client.

"Just get me out," Triple J said, while standing to his feet and walking out of the attorney booth.

"I've never failed you, Mr. Johnson. I promise I won't fail you now," T.J. yelled at the glass window.

Back in the cell, Triple J laid stretched out on the bunk drunk with anger.

"No bond tomorrow. Damn, I need a drink," he said to himself. Bugg had told him downstairs to put on his seat belt.

"You in for a ride with that murder case, shawty," his homeboy said.

The only person Triple J knew could make him feel better was wifey. Pulling his phone from his inside pocket he had sown inside the waistband, Triple J called Jessica.

"Yes, Big Daddy!" she answered joyfully, while holding her nose.

"What's up, Mama. I see you're having a good day," Triple J said.

"Yes, I been waiting all day to hear from you."

"I'm sorry. You know I hate to keep MeMa waiting,"

Triple J said, calling her by her pet name he had created for her.

"Yea, that's why tomorrow needs to hurry up so I can get you out of there."

Triple J looked up high into the corners of the cell. He didn't know how to tell her, but he knew he had to.

"I just saw T.J., MeMa and it's not looking good right now. He said I got secretly indicted and I won't be able to get a bond until next month, no later than ninety days."

"That's bullshit!" Jessica blurted out angrily.

Triple J knew she was really upset without him because she'd never been the type to curse, she was usually always getting on him.

"There are so many words you can use in the English language to get your point across other than curse words," she once said to him, but not now. She was right. It was bullshit.

Jessica immediately began crying as Triple J tried to comfort her over the phone, but it led to her sobbing. Destroyed mentally hearing his wife cry her soul out, he couldn't take it anymore and hung up.

Being a husband, my job is to keep my wife happy, he thought to himself. *It hurts so bad that I can't."*

Triple J laid the phone down on the bed and cried his eyes out. Although he didn't wanna look weak in front of Flamez, he had to because, Shit Just Got Real.

26

*A*ll night long, Triple J laid across the bunk, thinking how he could make things right for his wife. All Jessica wanted right now was her husband and all he wanted was for her to be happy. Not really a religious person, Triple J tried to find refuge and began to pray.

"Father God, if you can hear me, hey. I don't know what to say or how to introduce myself, but I'm James Johnson, Junior. Everyone calls me Triple J. I know it's inappropriate to come to you in a time like this, but the way I see it, anytime is a good time to come and you should be happy that I came, because I really don't know what to believe in right now other than myself.

Pop always told me you have a bigger purpose for my life than the ones right now. And I really don't understand, but I'm coming to you right now in need. My wife is hurting, and I can't help her. My old man always uses the word's purpose and says that you have a bigger purpose for my life.

I wanna know what it is. If you can help me through this situation and help me find my purpose, I appreciate you. I'm willing to do that, but I just need for you to make sure my wife is happy. I appreciate that and I appreciate you. Alright, I'll holla at you soon. Amen," Triple J closed out, feeling some sense of relief.

Triple J knew the Fulton jail had a habit of fucking up. Last week, the local news reported how they had mistakenly transported the wrong guy to prison who was supposed to be released and released the guy who was recently convicted for triple homicide. On a revenge streak when they let him out, he went and killed the entire household of one of his trial witnesses' family before killing himself.

That couldn't have been a coincidence, Triple J thought with his hand on his chin. *If God is in control of everything and it's all been written before our birth, he had to know that man was gone get out and kill them folks. The new question is why?*

A tap on the cell window caused both, Triple J and Flamez, to look up from their bunks.

"Johnson, you have court in the morning," the officer said, piercing through the window at him. "I'll be back to get you at four, so try to get you some rest," he continued.

Triple J looked at him and nodded his head, signaling okay even though he already knew he was supposed to go.

The ride to court was very uncomfortable for the crime boss. He was placed in shackles and chains, hands cuffed to the back with waist chains attached.

"Watch your step gentleman as you all step off," the transport Sargent said as everyone stepped on the Prisoner Transport Bus.

Triple J took a seat in the middle, not wanting to sit in the far back of the bus for the sake of Rosa Parks. And also believed sitting in the middle would be generous to the guys with disabilities.

Even though he actually wasn't having court today, he was glad to take the ride. On the bus he was surrounded by about five or six of his lil apes and cubs and they were all placed in the same holding tank inside.

"Triple J!" Ape Shit Jack his lil ape from intake called out. "I heard you got the 7th floor fucked up big homie. They say you eating good up there," he continued super excited.

Hearing about the move Triple J made had him piped up but that was nothing to the crime boss. Time had passed since he been around the young apes and now he realized how much they really needed his presence.

"These lil homies got potential to be great. They just needed some jewels dropped on them," Triple J said to himself.

"Yeah, Jack. You know everything legit. We go Ape shit everywhere. We go Ape Shit, Jack. But real shit, cell phones, weed, and cigarettes, that's small. Nothing to get excited over. We're all up there facing life sentences making Buick money. The real money is on the outside. We can laugh and act an ass when we all having Bentley money and getting brain from a big booty freak in the back seat. You ever rode in a Bentley?" Triple J asked him.

"Hell naw, but I want to."

"To live like money, you gotta get money. In order to get money, you gotta understand money, just like you know this gang shit. Your knowledge is your lit. Use this time to get you some financial lit like *Think and Grow Rich* by Napoleon Hill, *48 Laws of Power* by Robert Greene, or *The Personal MBA* by Josh Haufman.

When we all get a billion dollars a piece, then we going

Ape shit. When we get our own ANW TV network like Bob Johnson, the founder of BET, then we going Ape shit. Petty hustling in a jail ain't shit, Jack. Nothing to get excited over and I apologize for even bringing that shit in here. Trapping is exactly what it is. A TRAP!

We're all from the streets and got all the skills to survive anywhere. I wanna see all my Apes and Wolves sitting in Silicon Valley boardrooms, closing deals with major tech companies. I wanna see us side by side in private jets flying back getting brain with billions in our accounts," Triple J continued to encourage them.

Ape Shit Jack and the rest of the crew shook their heads vigorously, agreeing as they listened.

"Y'all got more power and equipment at your disposal to be whatever you wanna be. I'm down here facing life and might be gone for a long while," he said, pausing to take a breath. "I need y'all to step up and go ape shit in the corporate offices, not the county," he continued to speak, pointing at them individually.

Triple J shook everyone's hand and bumped heads with them. At that exact moment, his prayer was answered, and he learned his purpose.

Shit Just Got Real.

27

*T*hings had become a mess while Triple J was away at court. OG Big Boo, thanked God he walked in at the time he did because shit was about to get real. Once again, ANW and Blood Gang counterparts were at it. Both sides, standing with knives drawn and sinister looks in their eyes. Triple J, not knowing the situation, stepped in quickly calling for OG Big Boo to have a sit down with him at the dayroom table for a second time.

"I see our agreement has taken a malicious turn," Triple J said, breaking the silence.

"Yeah, on your part," OG Big Boo said angrily with his shoulders flared up. "The agreement was between me and you. Not that nigga Flamez," he said very upset, looking over at Triple J's second in command.

"I apologize for the misunderstanding. When I speak, it's on behalf of all of ANW. ONE is ALL and ALL is ONE. Flamez is my second in command in here and I trust him with my life. I was scheduled for a court hearing today and would have gotten out on bond if I wasn't indicted, so I prearranged for him to take on everything so that when I do leave, things could continue as we agreed."

"Yea, fuck all that. I deal with you, not Flamez or anybody else," OG Big Boo yelled.

Triple J stared at him in silence, thinking to himself that OG Big Boo had serious issues. Especially if he thought Triple J was going to continue to allow him to yell this way.

His ego got him feeling like he's the big man and he actually is in his organization in jail. Little does he know, he's an under boss. I'm the HNIC, the Head Nigga In Charge, everywhere," Triple J thought to himself.

Triple J saw where he was trying to take it, because he knew, he knew how to play the game.

"We are lead chairs in the community whether we like it or not, we have to work together to keep the community intact. If you, for some reason, are absent, I have no issue with working with the next man that steps up. I'm a man of my word and to keep my word, I appointed someone to fill my place just in case I one day become absent. ANW is ALL for ONE and ONE for ALL. When you see me you see us," Triple J said, dropping big homie jewels on him.

Although Triple J was talking, at the same time, he was reading OG Big Boo's body language. In his heart, he felt the high level of envy he had towards him and knew that would become an issue.

"Now he's ego tripping, creating problems like a little kid would. Thinking he would get a cookie for good behavior. Not in this lifetime," Triple J thought to himself.

Knowing he was egotistical, Triple J bossed up and offered him an opportunity he couldn't refuse.

"On this drop, I saw where our shortcomings came from. We got the seventh floor on lock, but a lot of money was left on the sixth that we missed. If you move down to the sixth, we can take over the entire jail. We need this because neither one of us has a trustworthy member from our team down there that can move product like that for us on this next drop. The numbers are still going to be the same, but on this one, I got a half bag for you. Send me two back off of it."

One thing the drug game taught Triple J when he was young was that good dope sold itself. A half-pound of Christmas trees for $2,000 was a steal and OG Big Boo knew that.

"Okay, cool," he replied excitedly. "How we gone get down there?" OG Big Boo asked Triple J.

"Remember, I'm Mr. Make It Happen. Now, let's get this money," Triple J said, dapping him.

Shit Just Got Real.

28

*F*or the next couple of months, Triple J vowed to himself to take care of his big homie responsibilities now that he had found his purpose. In a semicircle, his guys in the dormitory gathered around him with facial expressions of pure amazement. They were excited to be with the Don Dada. His presence was something they could all brag about for the rest of their lives.

In the ANW, he passed down literature aka Lit. These were stories on how ANW came about. For Triple J to get them to understand today, he had to take them back to when it all began.

"Originally, we were just the Grant Park Apes," he began, giving them his firsthand history lesson. "Everybody from Grant Park had a rep for going Level 3, Mental Health," he said, beating across his chest as he talked, "When guys from the other side came through the hood on that bullshit, we went ape shit. And that's how the name Grant Park Apes came about. It fit us perfectly because right in the center of our hood sat the Atlanta Zoo, infamously known for its

Silverback Gorilla Exhibit," Triple J continued and several of them shook their heads in agreement.

"The Wolves were from the west side. They used to trap off Simpson and Ashby. But their meet up spot was Washington Park. Every Sunday night when the whole city came together, everybody would meet at the Metro Bowling Alley and they would be deep just like us. It felt like you was at the ATL Trap Awards. The parking lot looked like a police auction, trap rides everywhere. Everybody rode rimmed up, 30" chrome tennis shoes on the rides," Triple J said smiling as he reminisced.

"When we walked in, it was with so many people that you would think the New York Thanksgiving Day Parade was going on. Usually the Wolves posted on the other side of the building, but one night, Lil Thug Thugga was in the building and the promoters sectioned the Wolves spot off for him and his crew. Everybody just knew that night, it was gone be a real issue when they ended up on the same side as us. I was standing on the sofas like I always did," Triple J said and laughed.

"And one of the Wolves thought he was the weatherman, throwing money in the air. Now I didn't have no problem with him making it rain until that shit fell on me," Triple J said, brushing off his shoulder. "Y'all know I wasn't going for that. I had to do something because, if not, one of my Apes was gone go ape shit and that's what they expected from us, but we had become rich by then. King JT Wolf was just JT Wolf then and there was no way in the hell I was gone let him outshine us. I had DJ Plug turn on that Jeezy song, "I Put On for My City", and we went ape shit with the Bag.

Everybody already knew Grant Park Apes had the bag. We would travel with The Mula Team and whenever Floyd came to the city. The traps back then jumped around the clock. So sometimes after a major pick up, I would travel with the money bag. That night I did. When I reached in, I grabbed three 100k rubber band blocks, broke them down, and passed it all out. Stacks went around to all my Apes to go ape shit.

He had hit me with some one's, but we was throwing twenties, fifties and hundreds. Before I knew it, money covered the floor and girls were dancing around us. We had a strip show in the bowling alley and put on for our city," Triple J continued with a smile.

"We had so much money on the floor that a money mound covered my shoes. The crowd was going crazy, females were running all around us, picking the money up. It was like we were paying a hood tax. King JT was playa about the situation. He recognized who the real boss in the city was and found his way over next to me.

'What up, doe?' he said, speaking like he was from Detroit.

"What's hannin', shawty," I kicked back at him, talking my ATL shit.

"You know that Ape Shit cool, but Wolves, we rule," he said.

"Naw, you got the game all wrong, homie. Y'all wolves are cool, and everybody know this Ape shit rules, even you." I said to him, "We shook hands, merging both crews and formed ANW, The Apes and Wolves.

When we linked, we got closer than a grieving family. The movement took off so fast and numbers grew so quickly, it started to seem unreal. On the last count, we was 2600 strong in the streets," Triple J said, wowing them. "We grew so fast, we had to establish a ranking system and still break down into two teams. The Money Team and The Hunters Team," Triple J said as they shook their heads up and down now that they understood.

"Everybody was about getting money, but we got money in different ways. So, The Money Team was all our hustlers, trapping it out, slanging cane. And the Hunters Team were our enforcers."

The Baby Apes and Cubs from the hood grew up seeing how we were getting money and they started screaming ANW the loudest. We were running the streets already but when Wild Child Wolf wrote his hit song and the radio picked it up, we went viral."

We got waves spinning, We jays spending,
Too much money in these pockets, big o'l bank spilling,
State to State spending, Switching lanes spinning,
Home Run 9th inning bitch we all winning
Winning, winning, winning,
ANW winning, winning, winning
Winning, winning, winning
ANW winning, winning,.

"Y'all know the dance they had to go with the song?" Triple J asked.

Three of them started to hit the money dance, rocking their knees from side to side with their hands held like they were holding sacks.

"Y'all seen how I made sure they went ape shit in the videos. It was over a million dollars in cars, jewelry, clothes, and girls. We had to show the world we was winning. My Israelite friend, Alen, owns six of the major clubs in Atlanta and every time somebody big comes to perform, he makes sure ANW Wild Child Wolf performs. One night Ricky Rossie came out and had MBG Meek with him to perform. They came to put on, but really didn't know what to do after the opening act. When ANW hit the stage, we threw 100k in the crowd while Wild Child Wolf performed the "Winning" song and shit went viral. While Rossie was on stage performing after we stepped off, he paused to call us up there with him. He took off one of his MBG chains and said, 'Triple J, you're the Biggest Boss,' and put it on my neck. He took off another one and put it on Wild Child Wolf's neck and said, 'You're next to blow.' That night, ANW was trending. TZM Celebrity News aired the tape and we went viral all over social media. The after party was at the MBG Mansion and that's where Rossie offered me the 10.5-million-dollar joint venture deal for Wild Child Wolf and a 50/50 deal on whoever else we signed. With the big music connections to take ANW worldwide, the city saw that, and everybody knew then, Shit Just Got Real.

29

"*L*ock down, gentleman. Lock down," the Sargent said as he walked through the 100 door. "Trays will be up shortly."

"Fuck them trays. We winning in here," one of the young apes screamed as he walked up the stairs.

Everybody in the dorm laughed, even the Sarge, because he too knew what was going on. They were really winning. It wasn't a cell without at least $30 worth of commissary inside.

Triple J laughed but was really thankful for how far he had come.

Growing up in the Grant Park community was difficult for them. They ran constantly from the police when they were hungry after stealing from the store, right across from the precinct. Most of their meals came from school. When they did eat at home, it was mayonnaise sandwiches or ketchup burgers. One piece of bread folded in half, no meat, no pickle, and all ketchup or mayonnaise.

The jail food wasn't good at all and most of the time

when they did get it on the seventh floor, it was either cold or hard. There was no such thing as flavor or seasoning.

Triple J remembered where he came from and vowed, "No matter how much money I get, I will never say nothing bad about any food unless it's spoiled."

After lock down, Triple J and Flamez went over the money together. A few of the numbers didn't look right and needed to be cleared up.

"The sales from the 5th to 7th floor need to see an increase," Triple J told Flamez. "I'm sending OG Big Boo down to the 6th and turn him loose down there to get out our way," Triple J continued.

Flamez nodded his head up and down because he too was tired of the back and forth beef between the two groups.

When all was understood, Triple J turned Flamez loose and let him do his thang while he went and booed up with wife.

"Jessie, what's up, baby?" he said when she answered the phone.

"This some bullshit. I hate the whole DA's office," she said, pouting and still upset he didn't get a bond.

Triple J knew she was sad, living in their big house alone every night. It hurt him so bad because he was used to giving her everything she wanted and right now, he couldn't even give her a hug. The only thing he knew that could change things around was God.

"*A family that prays together, stays together,*" he remembered his father telling him.

Jessica, a devout Christian, recited the Serenity's Prayer with him.

"God give us the strength to accept the things we cannot change, the courage to change the things that we can, And the wisdom to know the difference. Amen."

When they finished, she sniffled a couple of times, then bust out laughing.

"Daddy, I love you so much. You always make my sadness go away."

"Not me, God did that," he said, taking none of the credit with the little faith that he had.

For several hours, they talked before it started getting late. Triple J asked her to come see him the next day and she promised she would.

What she didn't know was that since they'd been on the phone, he had ordered an edible arrangements basket. Delivery time was in the morning at 8AM. It would be his treat for her treat.

Pineapples, Triple J thought as he processed the order.

The breakfast trays were on the way, so Triple J and Flamez put everything up. Flamez began telling Triple J about his old lady. She was glad they were roommates because since Triple J came in the picture he'd been able to take care of the house.

One of ANW's sayings is, "Take care of the house first, and the house will take care of you."

Triple J always told his closest associates, "Any man that don't take care of home can never consider himself The Man because he's not even manning his own home."

While they were laying down talking, a surprise visitor

hit the door.

"Both of y'all get up and cuff up," Officer Williams said as he flashed his light into their cell. "I ain't playing. Get up and come cuff up," he continued.

Officer Williams was what they called a super cop in the jailhouse. Everyone assumed he had no life outside of there, because he did the most when he got to work.

Triple J and Flamez knew what he was coming to do—shake down their cell, but they weren't worried because everything was already put up.

"I hope you make Sargent, fucking with us this early in the morning," Flamez said, taunting him. "You know we ain't got shit you just wanna fuck with somebody."

Officer Williams, an entry level detention officer, checked under their mats first. Triple J and Flamez watched from outside of their cell as he pulled out a silver tool with a red handle.

With a smirk on his face, he climbed on top of the toilet and then on top of the sink before he unscrewed the screws from their light. Triple J looked at Flamez and wondered how he knew to check the light.

"I tightened the screws back tight," Flamez mouthed to him.

"I know," Triple J said.

After Flamez put everything up, Triple J checked behind him to make sure they weren't loose.

When Officer Williams took out the last nut, he pulled the light cover out and dug his hand behind the metal plate. When he started pulling everything out, Triple J got pissed. Officer Williams knew he was in the wrong spot, but he smirked like he was a hero.

Shit Just Got Real.

30

alking with his chest out like he had just won the Georgia Lottery, Officer Williams taunted Triple J about his find. Little did he know, the ticket he cashed in was the wrong one and the rightful owner had different plans for him.

As they were escorted out of the dorm, Triple J and Flamez were split up. Flamez went to 700 and Triple J went to 800 followed by Officer Williams.

"Johnson, I know those your phones," Officer Williams said to him.

Triple J, an already experienced inmate with the law, ignored him and began walking along the rec wall.

"What is it with these Williams boys," Triple J asked himself, remembering ACP, Officer J. Williams, who also gave him a hard time.

"I hit the Jackpot tonight," he continued, stepping around Triple J, cutting him off.

Triple J looked Officer Williams in the face and laughed.

Officer Williams immediately got upset that Triple J's

wasn't intimidated and grabbed hold of his restrained arm. With brute force, he spun Triple J around and threw his back against the wall.

"Johnson, let's go," Captain James yelled, standing with Lt. Rodgers at the rec yard's entrance.

Blood boiling hot, Triple J was glad to see the Captain, but wished more he was not cuffed. Snatching away from the ignorant officer's grip, Triple J walked towards their direction.

Captain James grabbed his right arm and Lt. Rodgers grabbed the left. Officer Williams followed them out and Captain James snapped.

"Go on to 700 until I get back," Captain James yelled at him. "You had no fucking business going into that cell alone. And you don't even have a camera on making the search, no good Rookie!" the Captain continued.

Williams' face turned sour and his cheers of joy were lost. Although he found the jackpot, Fulton jail had a policy that when an officer shook down a cell, they must have their body camera on.

Triple J wasn't that worried about the phones he found because he knew they were no good without the sims card held in his mouth.

Towards the elevators they walked and Triple J knew exactly where they were going.

Inside the administrative offices, Triple J turned to Captain James.

"Ya mans fucked up big time, Captain," Triple J told him.

"That's already handled, Johnson. Don't worry about him," Lt. Rodgers said, trying to calm the upset Triple J.

"How you let him knock you, Johnson?" Captain James asked.

"I didn't let him do SHIT! Everything was already locked up. The man snuck through the side door, opened our cell door with the key and said 'cuff up.' Like I said, everything was put up, so we weren't too worried about him coming in. First, he flipped up the mattresses up, then checked around the room before he climbed on the toilet and started fucking with the light. He pulled out a red screwdriver and started to open it. I'm still not worried about it because you know that light has a star nut on it. When he started twisting and they started coming out, I knew then shit had just got real! It was like he knew where everything was at."

The three of them walked into the Captain's office and took a seat. Captain James logged into the computer, pulling up Omari Williams's HR file. The printer began spitting out multiple pages. Captain James grabbed them and set it on his desk so Triple J could see the information. While Triple J looked down, Captain James typed away at his computer and turned the screen around.

"Last night, two off duty Fulton jail corrections officers were gunned down as they pulled into their driveways after leaving work," the female reporter said, getting Triple J's attention.

He looked up at Captain James as she continued and watched with no emotions.

"Please let us handle this. We already have to bury two of our own. We don't need a third," the Captain said when the story finished.

"Death comes in threes,'" Triple J said. "He knows what he is doing."

The captain knew exactly what he meant. He looked down at the HR file and back at Triple J. Captain James knew the crime boss was no slouch and wished the heat had not come down on the department. He also knew Triple J could have done it a lot more quietly but chose to make a statement.

Lt Rodgers saw things were going south and knew she could use her charm to change Triple J's mind.

"Captain, I'm gone take Johnson to my office and do a little interrogation of my own with him," she said.

"Y'all hurry along and don't be too long, we got a shift coming in." Both individuals were stressed and needed relief. As Lt. Rodgers walked out, Triple J followed her.

"Hell yeah," he said, looking at her backside twist as they walked out. "I really need to get topped off right now, bae," he said as he followed.

As soon as she closed the office door behind them, everything went into go mode.

"You heard the Captain. Pull that dick out," she said, making demands.

Triple J laughed at her, but he did what she said.

Sluuurrrpp.

She sounded off with her mouth, sucking in Triple J. She pulled her head back, making a popping sound and he smiled. Lt. Rodgers made her head bobble up and down, sucking Triple J good until he was about to cum. As his legs tightened up, he planned to bust in her mouth until she stopped.

"I know damn well you didn't forget the rules. I gotta get mines before you get yours," she said, standing up and dropping her brown uniform pants.

Lt. Rodgers climbed onto Triple J's lap in reverse cowgirl, and took off riding. As she was going, Triple J felt like he was back at Magic City getting a table dance the way she twerked on his dick. Each time she came down the pole, a ripple shot back across her bubble butt.

Triple J drove deep inside of her, slapping her ass at times. She was going crazy on the pole like a rodeo rider while he gave her the big buck, long back shot.

Lt. Rodgers squirted for the first time and cum ran down Triple J's legs. He continued beating in her guts until he got what he came for.

"Boom," he blasted off and shot his cum deep inside of her.

She climbed off, smiling, and wiping him down with wipes from her desk drawer.

"Let us handle, Williams," Lt. Rodgers said as she continued to wipe him. "He gone get dealt with. Trust me, you'll see," she assured him.

"Aite, y'all got it."

The hallways were quiet as they headed back to Captain James's office. They assumed no one was there and Captain James was on the bull shit.

"I said I gotta get mines before you get yours. Now you gave me yours," Lt Rodgers said to Triple J.

"You right. You was supposed to swallow anyways," he replied, laughing with her.

"Maybe next time.'"

Lt. Rodgers looked at Triple J and licked her lips.

"It won't be no next time," a female's voice said, interrupting them.

Stepping out of Captain James's office was Triple J's wife, Jessica. Both of her hands were balled into tight fists as she came around the door frame. Neither of them knew who she was coming for, but one thing they did know was, Shit Just Got Real.

"*I* see you doing you already, James Johnson Junior," she said, upset, calling him by his whole name.

"Lieutenant Rodgers, this is my wife, Jessica. Jessica, this is—"

"I don't wanna meet this bitch," Jessica snapped "You the same hoe that was looking at me crazy a couple weeks ago in court," Jessica said, snapping at Lt. Rodgers.

She was pissed off and angry, but Jessica had every right to be. Although no mirror was there, Triple J stared at himself.

"Here I am living like I'm a single man, giving up what belongs to my wife. Although Lt Rodgers is a Sheriff Deputy, she still is nothing but a groupie on my dick for the hype," he thought to himself.

Captain James saw how things were about to turn and stepped in between them, guiding Jessica back into his office with Triple J. On the sofa, Jessica sat with her arms folded breathing heavily.

"You thank fucking that bitch was the right thang?" she asked him. "Come on now, James. Be for fucking real," Jessica continued upset.

"No!" Triple J said to her.

"I'm working day and night for you, James. For us and our brand and this is how you do me?" Jessica said with tears forming in her eyes. "I used to feel loved, but now I know you're ungrateful."

Her words were gut wrenching to Triple J's ears. All he could think was, *"I don't wanna lose my wife, especially with all we got going on."*

Crippling tears ran from her eyes, hurting him more than anything could. Jess tried to speak, but her words were unclear.

"I couldn't hear you. Say it one more time," he said.

"James, I'm pregnant!" she screamed. Triple J looked down, staring at her stomach and thought, *"damn."*

Shit Just Got Real.

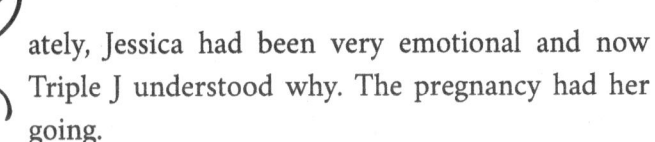ately, Jessica had been very emotional and now Triple J understood why. The pregnancy had her going.

"When did you find out?" Triple J asked her.

"My cycle was supposed to start four days ago, but it didn't. So, I bought one of those pharmacy test kits, and it showed positive," she said.

For months, they'd been putting in work for Baby James. It wasn't an unexpected occurrence for the couple, but surely they'd rather it not be under these circumstances.

Excited as much as he could be, Triple J cringed at the thought of being an expecting father, with an unknown future. He was uncertain how the next couple of months would play out, let alone the next couple of years. The thought of serving a life sentence crossed his mind.

"How am I supposed to be a father serving a life sentence," he asked himself, *"How am I supposed to celebrate my child's first birthday?"*

Reality hit him hard, he felt a sharp pain through his chest. Triple J began to realize that he might not ever get to meet his child's school teachers, high school sweetheart or even be there to send him or her off to college.

Jessica continued to cry. Triple J interrupted her tear tracks, planting kisses all over her face.

"Baby, we did it!" he said, overly excited with a huge smile ripping the side of his face. "Have you told your father yet?" Triple J asked.

Ever since they'd been married, the mayor had been asking for a grandson and Triple J promised to give him one.

"Not yet. I came to tell you first," she said, exchanging her tears for a smile.

"How does it feel? Do you feel different inside? Like can you feel him growing already?"

"No, fool!" Jessica said, slapping her hand against his arm. "I'm not that far along yet," she continued.

"I'm sorry," Triple J said. "You know I don't know, baby. This our first time. I don't know how this goes. I always got other folks' kids pinned on me. 'Triple J, I need some pampers for your child.' 'When you gone come see your child?' I never knew I had one," he said, mimicking the young women he dated before Jessica. "But the one thing I know for sure is he's mines," he said, leaning over kissing Jessica's stomach.

A double tap on the door interrupted them.

"Excuse me," Captain James said. "May I come in?"

"Come on, Captain," Triple J said. He and Jessica were just sitting on the sofa together.

"Mrs. Johnson," Captain James said, bowing his head in respect for her. "I apologize I couldn't speak to you earlier. I thought I was gonna have to peel you off your husband's ass."

Jessica laughed and looked at Triple J, shaking her head up and down.

"Mmmhmm, he was about to get his ass kicked all across that hallway."

Triple J laughed because he knew she couldn't kick his ass. He'd been studying Wing Chun martial arts since he was eight years old. Never would he raise his hand to hit his wife under any circumstances, but he knew she wouldn't get past his defense. His block game was so good, she would get frustrated with herself because she wouldn't be able to hit him. Still, it was entertaining to hear, Triple J thought.

"Say, Captain, I don't think you would have been able to get her off by yourself. I haven't been able to break her grip since we met. I love my wife. she's the best thing to ever come into my life," he said, staring deep into her eye's.

"Yes, sir. Mr. Johnson, you do have an amazing wife with a very powerful father," he said, referring to the Mayor.

"Yes, my father is pretty cool," Jessica replied.

"Speaking of him, how is he?" Captain James asked.

"He's wonderful. I spoke with him this morning on his way to the office," she answered.

"Good! Well, tell him Captain James is taking good care of his son and daughter down here next time you talk with him."

"Mr. Johnson, is it okay for us to speak now?" Captain James asked, referring to Jessica's presence in the room.

"Yes sir," Triple J answered with certainty.

One thing he knew was that Jessica was super official. Anything said to him, could be said in front of her without a worry of leaking.

"This evening when Officer Williams reports to work, our K-9 unit will be outside. Your man Flamez wanted to take the charge, but I'm going to work it out for him so that he doesn't. Williams is going to be arrested for drug possession and crossing the guard lines with illegal substances. A package is being prepared for you right now for our officers' inconvenience to you, Mr. Johnson. He will be processed later this evening into the jail and given a bond out. Neither of us can stand the heat right now, so please allow us to handle him," Captain James asked.

Triple J wasn't planning to wipe him out, but a message needed to be sent. Lt. Rodgers and Captain James asked him to let them handle it, so Triple J agreed.

"Yes sir, Captain. I give you my word on my baby boy," Triple J said, rubbing on Jessica's stomach.

"Congratulations!" Captain James said, smiling as he looked down at Jessica's stomach. "Your package will be up there later today."

"Thank you," Jessica said, smiling.

"I have to get him back upstairs. Mrs. Johnson. Don't worry about him. I got it. He'll be back online in a couple hours."

On the elevator back to the 7th floor, Triple J asked Captain James to make the move for him with OG Big Boo and his crew. The Captain gave him his word that he would make the move happen today. This was something Triple J needed to make everything go smoothly.

In the cell, he laid down to get his head right. As he was dozing off, Officer Grant, the mail lady, came in.

"Mail Call, mail call, mail call," she screamed. "Johnson, you got mail," she said, smiling through the cell window.

Since coming in through the back gate, Triple J had been getting an abundance of mail. Mainly from people he didn't know. Cards, letters, pictures. Even a request to film a movie documentary covering his life.

Triple J was one of Ms. Grant's regulars, stopping by his cell several times a week. Triple J climbed off the rack and met her at the door.

"Congratulations," she said as she passed him the letters under the door.

"Congratulations," he said to himself, wondering how she knew he and Jess were expecting when he just found out.

The top envelope he received was from an Ashleigh "Flyya" Tucker. Triple J had no idea who she was but pulled the inside line paper out and began reading the letter.

Dear, Baby Daddy.

How are you holding up in there? You may be wondering who I am and why I'm calling you baby daddy, but I'm the flight attendant you met on your way back to Atlanta. I saw something special in you before I ever knew who you were. A tall, handsome, black man with thick wavy hair. I instantly fell in love with the man I had seen. We did something that I've never done before and I wanna thank you for the experience. I looked you up and saw that you're married but I don't care. I didn't care then. I don't care now because I don't mind being a co-wife.

At first I wasn't sure. I thought it was just an upset stomach that made me vomit, until my urine test results came back and my doctor said I was pregnant.

What I'm trying to tell you is that I'm carrying your seed. I wanted you to know so I don't seem like some groupie whore pinning her child on you after she's born. This is something we have together, and I promise to make it last forever and ever. Don't be a stranger.

Your Second Wife,
Ashleigh

Triple J read the letter for a second time and then a third. All he could think now was damn, Shit Just Got Real.

33

"*When is it gonna get better,*" Triple J asked himself after reading Ashleigh's pregnancy's letter.

Ever since he got that call from his father, while in Texas, his life had been all out of whack. The thoughts of incarceration crossed his mind, but not to this extent. There was no way the crime boss could have prepared himself for any of this, from success to murder arrest. James and Jessica had now become James, Jess, Ashleigh, and two babies on the way.

With a child outside of his marriage, Triple J didn't know how things were going to go. He wondered constantly how he was going to explain things to his wife when she'd just caught him cheating with Lt. Rodgers here at the jail. Triple J tried to gather himself, but it seemed like more and more stress engulfed him. He closed his eyes and tried relaxation exercises he had seen online.

"Take a deep breath and hold it for ten seconds, Exhale slowly," he remembered the relaxation coach saying.

Every time he exhaled, he said, "Let go and let God."

Falling into a state of relaxation, Triple J found a sense of comfort, but it didn't last long.

"Triple J!" Officer Price, the coolest male officer in the jail, called him by his moniker over the intercom. "You have an attorney visit in booth five."

"Thank you, God. It's time to go," Triple J said out loud.

Quickly, he jumped up and threw on his blue jumpsuit uniform. Even though he had the best-looking two-piece scrubs in the jail, Triple J wanted his attorney to see him how he felt— bad!

Maybe T.J. would work harder to get me out," he thought as he got dressed. Quickly, Triple J shot out of the dorm to 700 where the visitation booths were after Officer Price opened his cell from the booth.

Seated at the officers' desk, beautiful as always, was Deputy Kelly. The word around the jail was that she was a full-time model outside of work. She had the curvature and smile to definitely fit the description of a magazine cover girl. Every time she saw Triple J, she showed off that million-dollar smile, blushing. She knew Triple J had taken a liking to her and before he could say anything flirtatious, she shot him a curve.

"Your attorney is waiting upstairs for you upstairs in booth five, Mr. Johnson," she said, showing off her bright smile.

Triple J stumbled steps towards her, then pointed in the direction of the stairs and walked towards them.

"Thank you, Ms. Concierge," he said, flirting with her anyways.

They stared at each other, eyes locked his entire way up

the stairs. The moment was magical, until he reached the last step and stumbled.

"Don't fall," she said, giggling at him flirtatiously.

"I fell when I first locked eyes on you," Triple J replied smooth and cool.

The giggles of a third grader came from Deputy Kelly this time. She had to catch her glasses from falling off her face because she was laughing so hard.

"Take your behind in there and talk with your lawyer," she said to him as he walked up to booth five.

T.J. stood from his chair and laid down his legal pad when Triple J walked in.

"It's good to see you today, my friend," Triple J said to his attorney. "What's the deal?"

T.J. held out his hand towards the stool on Triple J's side of the glass.

"Please, have a seat, Mr. Johnson. I have some important things to go over with you," T.J. said.

"I know you got something good for me, T.J. Things have been going bad for me all day," Triple J told him. "I just found out this morning I have two babies on the way. And it's not good."

"The wife's having twins?" he asked excitedly.

"No, I fucked up," Triple J said, holding his head down. "On the way here from Texas, I smashed the flight attendant on the plane. I got a letter from her today stating she's pregnant. I know it's very possible because I did buss in her."

T.J. stared at him in thought.

"Well Mr. Johnson, these are new problems, but they are all meant to be solved."

T.J. was good at his job, but Triple J thought this was one that he needed to handle on his own. If it was true that the two babies were his, only a real man would do what he had to do to be the best father he could from behind the fence.

"That's serious but we have more serious issues. The ADA filed a motion seeking the death penalty."

T.J.'s words were like three armor piercing rounds, shooting through Triple J's chest and out his back.

"The death penalty," he repeated, while grabbing a hold of his chest.

The chest pains he'd been feeling stabbed him heavily and Triple J grabbed a hold of the stainless-steel desk in front of him with his free hand.

"Yes, Mr. Johnson. I know. It all shocked me when I got the news. That's why I came straight down here."

"How can they seek the death penalty? I thought that was for shit like killing a cop. Or when you have multiple murders."

"Yes, that's true, Mr. Johnson. You were indicted on capital murder which is punishable by death," T.J. said.

This day couldn't get any worse t for the crime boss. He thought about the "Let Go and Let God" song, then came to the conclusion that there was no God.

As he sat there with T.J., the day's events replayed in his mind. First, it was Williams tearing his cell apart. Then it was Jessica catching him after he had smashed Lt. Rodgers. Then the news of Ashleigh's pregnancy from the letter that came in the mail. Now T.J. was telling him not only was he facing a life sentence, but it was possible he would be killed in prison by the needle or electric chair. Tears began to run down the face of the crime boss heavily and his chest pains grew stronger.

"What can we do, T.J.?" he asked with his hands pressed.

"James, we've moved many mountains together and as

your counselor, I have to tell the truth. Someone very powerful is behind this and they want you away for good. I have two federal criminal defense attorneys that are going to be assisting me with this. Your chances are slim, but our fight is on."

Triple J stood because he couldn't sit through this anymore. His heart began to beat faster and faster as T.J. talked before he walked off.

Yelling through the glass, T.J. tried to encourage him.

"Mr. Johnson, we're warriors. We fight the beast. Like David we have three stones to cast. Don't give up. We fight."

It sounded good and Triple J wanted to believe him, but he couldn't right now. His heart was beating faster and faster as he walked to the stairs.

T.J. continued to yell through the glass, but all Triple J could hear was, "The Death Penalty, The Death Penalty, The Death Penalty". It was replaying over and over in his head.

"How in the hell is Jessica going to take this," he thought to himself.

He looked over the handrail and saw Deputy Kelly still seated at her desk. As he began to walk down the stairs, it hit him again, "The Death Penalty". This time it knocked him unconscious.

Shit Just Got Real.

BREAKING NEWS

"We have breaking news for you outside of Atlanta's Memorial Hospital. Melissa are you there?," the news anchor asked, staring into the camera.

"Yes, John! I'm sorry, it's my earpiece. I can't hear you clear," Melissa said, fiddling under her hair.

"Yes! We're here reporting live to you outside of Atlanta's Memorial Hospital where it's been reported Atlanta Fire and Rescue EMT services were dispatched to the Fulton jail earlier today for an inmate unresponsive with a severe head injury and cardiac complications.

My sources say that when EMT arrived, that inmate was rushed here and quickly taken into the trauma center. Immediate attention was given to his injuries where he now lies in the intensive care unit.

When we got down here, our request for that inmate's identity was denied by hospital officials, but despite our extreme difficulties, we continued to investigate and learned right before airing our mystery man is the recently indicted murder suspect James "Triple J" Johnson, Junior.

For those of you that don't know, Mr. James Johnson, Junior is the son in law to our Atlanta Mayor Kaseem Reeves, husband to his daughter, Ms. Jessica Reeves-Johnson.

A couple weeks ago, my colleague, Isaac Snyder, covered a story on Johnson's arrest where he yelled into the camera he was innocent, and he loved his mama as he was being taken into the Atlanta's City Police Headquarters. Mr. Johnson was arrested in connection to the 2015 murder of Clarence "Little C" Coleman. He's not being accused of being the trigger man, but the guy who ordered the hit.

ACP detectives reported that during Mr. Johnson's arrest, that he is not the successful, law-abiding businessman we believed him to be. Instead, the ringleader of the well-known street gang, ANW, the Apes and Wolves, which have a reputation for extreme violence.

As of now, we're not sure how severe Mr. Johnson's condition is, but please stay tuned for an update on our WISN news app.

I'm Melissa Waters and this is Atlanta's number one local news station, WISN 2, where we get the news first and deliver it to you.

Back to you in the studio John."

"Thank you Melissa."

When Atlanta's Most Notorious crime boss and prominent businessman, Triple J, gets caught up in a murder investigation, his life takes a dive for the worst. Quickly he learns the Feds don't care who you are or where you are. When they get the call to get you, they're coming right then. Slammed to the floor while on vacation with his wife, Triple J also sang a familiar tune. "Please, sir. I can't breathe. I can't breathe," he said when one of the arresting officers used his knee and pressed it against his neck.

Luckily, he was able to live through the ordeal unlike many others in their police encounters. But once Triple J was hauled back to Atlanta and taken to the Fulton jail awaiting trial, he then realized how serious things were.

Shit Just Got Real.

ACKNOWLEDGMENTS

First, I wanna thank our creator for assisting me through this work of art and the Ancestors for guiding me along the way.

I wanna thank my father, spiritual adviser and business partner, for the encouragement and knowledge he's given me throughout my life, most of what I've passed on to you throughout this work of art.

I wanna thank my Big Brothers/Mentors, both published authors, Said M, Salaam and Deshion "Stack" Hightower, for the education and knowledge they've shared with me over the years. I promise to use it.

I wanna thank my assistant, CoCo, for the hours she's put in for all of this to come together.

My editor, Tisha Andrews and graphic designer, Adriane Hall, for our combination of expertise to bring this together.

My spiritual brother and marketing agent, V. Shanks @360marketing.

Triple salute to our U.S. Veterans, H. "Big D" Davis, J. "Big JB" Brooks, and the Devil Dog J. McCoy. You all helped me in so many ways along the way and encouraged me daily, asking, "How's the book coming. I can't wait to read it" and pointed me in the direction of self-publishing which helped me get the tools I needed to do so. Again, I Triple Solute you three and give thanks. Thank you for your services to our country.

My long list of family members, I won't list for security reasons, but I want you all too please know I love you dearly.

My son, my best friend, my little me. Daddy loves you, Baby Boy.

And, most of all, you, the readers. I thank you all and hope you enjoyed this book. Stay tuned for Part Two.

Love you all and God Bless.

Edited by Gaati Werema BA, MCD
Submitted 07/26/2022

DID YOU ENJOY THIS BOOK!

Shop with The Executive Homeboy and purchase your Shit Just Got Real Gear @ www. theexecutivehomeboy.com

Publishers/Authors Contact:
The Executive Homeboy
www.theexecutivehomeboy.com